DEEP ROOTS

Also by Beth Cato

DEEP ROOTS

BETH CATO

HARPER
VOYAGER
IMPULSE

An Imprint of HarperCollins Publishers

"The Deepest Poison." Copyright © 2015 by Beth Cato.
"Wings of Sorrow and Bone." Copyright © 2015 by Beth Cato.
"Final Flight." Copyright © 2016 by Beth Cato.

EPub Edition AUGUST 2016 ISBN: 9780062561572

Print Edition ISBN: 9780062561565

10 9 8 7 6 5 4 3 2

To my Grandma, with lots of zorbs.

CONTENTS

DEEP ROOTS

DEEP ROOTS

THE DEEPEST POISON

From my vantage point on the low crest, I knew Cantonment Five's situation had grown ominous since Miss Leander's missive had arrived in my hand some hours before.

The rising sun painted a sliver of horizon in the deep pink of a healing scar and illuminated the sprawl of the camp below. The whinnies of hungry horses carried at this distance even as the usual booms of shelling continued on the far side. Airships hovered above, like dark, ovoid clouds, though fewer were aloft than usual. No Caskentian army encampment should be so still.

Mercy upon us all if the front line fell. Wasters would be on us like ants on a crumb.

Captain Yancy, the commander of my escort party, conferred with the pickets on duty, their voices rushed. I caught the word "contagious" and immediately brought my horse around.

"It's not believed to be contagious," I said.

The guard held a fist to his chest in salute. Only his eyes were visible between the thick wrap of scarf and hat. "Miss Percival, m'lady, last I heard, a quarter of the men gone ill—"

A quarter of the men. That meant over two thousand. I schooled myself to remain stoic. "Miss Leander said this bore the marks of enteric illness. A matter of the bowels, food poisoning."

"I've been told not to eat or drink," he said.

"Good. Captain Yancy?"

We rode down the gradual slope to the cantonment with a heightened sense of urgency. I trusted Miss Leander's judgment else I would not have left her as matron at this vital base. I was still technically headmistress over her and about a dozen other medician women in training, all of us contracted by the Caskentian government to manage medical wards throughout the northern pass. With me were two of my trained medician girls, ten nurses of my hire, and a squadron of two hundred soldiers. The men were a concession of the Colonel at base camp; my midnight plea had only succeeded because the lout was fully drunk. A happy drunk, one easily coaxed by feminine smiles.

Captain Yancy rode alongside me. "M'lady, what should my men do?"

"Keep most of your men with me. We will require assistance in the wards."

"Whatever you need, Miss Percival."

I nodded. This old, prickled captain had not been so respectful toward me until recent months—not until, through the Lady's grace, I had spared him from multiple amputations. Worshipful officers were useful.

Army encampments always stank of dust and unwashed male bodies and manure, but this one now carried a strong acidic taint. Green-clad soldiers stood in the cold morning to watch as we rode past. Others staggered toward the wards, soaked in their own feculence. The quiet, the vulnerability of the place, unnerved me. I'd never seen the like in all my decades of intermittent service for the Caskentian army.

To the east of the Fair Valley of Caskentia, across the high peaks of the Pinnacles, sprawled desolate plains known as the Waste. During my childhood, the hardscrabble settlers of the Waste rebelled and kidnapped Caskentia's young princess. Her loss began a cycle of war that had continued, on and off, for some fifty years.

I dismounted and bit back a grunt as my stiff old legs met the hard ground. I unstrapped my satchel and draped it across my chest. The dull echoes of bomb blasts carried from nearby trench lines. With a motion to my medicians and nurses, I entered the reception tent.

My nostrils were bludgeoned by a foulness that cannot be described in proper company. The canvas tent was intended to house thirty swaddies, briefly, during triage. Now it was carpeted in a hundred bodies. Some moaned. Others were eerily still. An orderly waved a medician wand over a soldier. The crusted grime on him was immediately rendered to dust by the wand's enchantment, only for the patient to immediately soil himself again. Even so, efforts to sanitize were ongoing throughout the ward.

Despite the sheer numbers of ill men, all of them

wore proper triage tags on their boots. I couldn't help a surge in pride. While undeniably a crisis, the matter was being handled with proper compassion and decorum. This was precisely what I trained my girls for, why my academy existed.

A figure in a white dress and laden apron approached through the narrow path between patients, a satchel against her hip. The enchanted shimmer of Miss Leander's robes attracted the attention of most every conscious man in the room. All of my medicians were attired to be unblemished beacons of hope against the most dread of circumstances.

"Miss Percival!" Miss Leander's weary voice creaked, making her sound far older than her twenty-two years. Her head twitched, her attention jerked from side to side. Others might surmise she was overworked, which was true, but I'd known her for nearly ten years and knew she was acutely hearing the dismayed body songs of each dying soldier as she passed by.

Healing magi like us were a rarity. The Lady's Tree, a hidden wonder whose roots moored the world, had graced Miss Leander with healing skills far superior to my own. Even I required a sanctified circle to listen to a body's song and utilize special herbs to heal.

"Tell me the latest," I said.

"We've reserved bellywood bark treatment for moribund cases in operations, but as the sun's come up, many more men have been found ill," she said. Bellywood bark was blessed by the Lady to cure stomach and intestinal grief. Relying on the herb would have quickly saved more men, but our supplies were finite.

"You've relied on standard doctoring as long as possible. Good." I knew my praise pleased her. Though she was now a woman grown, she was still like a puppy around me, always in want of a scratch behind the ears.

"This new influx has shown us a pattern," she murmured. "The majority are from the northern side, so I believe the contamination's in water rather than food from the central tent."

"You haven't stated which enteric illness you believe this to be, Miss Leander."

She looked away, suddenly the shy pupil. Her brown hair, frazzled from the braids atop her head, lashed at her cheeks. "No. It doesn't . . . act or *sound* like typhoid, dysentery, or cholera. The music is distinct. Like no zyme I've heard before."

"How many men have died so far?"

"Thirty. No. Wait." She stopped and stooped over a soldier, then the one beside him. A wave of grief passed over her face. "Their songs are gone. Two more dead." As gifted and efficient as she was, she nursed guilt like a blotto with a bottle.

"Water contamination. Hmm. They draw from different water casks for the north and south sides here at Five, correct?"

"Yes. The tanks are full and functioning. I called for Sanitation Officer Wagner . . ." Her face went momentarily blank. "I'm not sure how long it's been now, I—"

I stopped her with an upraised hand. "Have the casks been inspected today?"

"I—no, not that I've been told—but I know there are medician rods installed to purify the river water—"

"Never assume," I said, sharper than intended. "Hundreds of men are ill. That implies taint at a larger source. We can't wait for this Officer Wagner. What of the base command?" I motioned her to follow me outside.

"I sent the Colonel to the operations theatre just before you arrived." She kept her voice low. "The Lieutenant Commander is now in charge, and in sound health last I heard."

"The Colonel was given priority in the medicians' queue, yes?"

"Yes." The tone was grudging. I granted her a nod of approval. In the past, she had tried to prioritize patients without mind to military rank. Caskentian soldiers were a barbarous, illiterate lot. Without proper chain of command to govern them, they were bumbling bumpkins.

"I'll quickly check on the Colonel myself." I turned toward the door. An orderly, walking backward, almost bowled me over as he hauled in a man.

"Outta the way! Miss Leander! We need you!" he cried.

My annoyance must have been obvious. Miss Leander shot me an apologetic look as she dashed over.

This was no time for me to call out the orderly on a breach of protocol, for ignoring me as the superior matron in the ward. I walked on, frowning. I always hated it when men in horrendous agony were forced to stand and salute for officers—this one little lapse shouldn't irritate me so.

The conditions within the operations ward were not as crowded though still quite wretched. I walked past the mundane surgeons' rooms to the medicians' segment of the chamber. It contained three large circles—ovals, really—made of one-inch copper bands embedded in the portable tile floor. Within each was an operating platform at waist level. The two girls I had brought along were busy at work. All three circles were activated, with healings in progress. The heat of the Lady's magic wafted over me. I breathed it in and, for an instant, knew peace, only for the stench of reality to return seconds later.

The Colonel's healing was at completion. The conducting medician was one I had hired to assist us at Cantonment Five. He nodded a greeting to me, and I stepped across the boundary of the circle. Magic draped over me as if I walked through a warm waterfall.

I could not walk through Miss Leander's circle boundaries. They were as solid as brick walls.

The Lady tended to all life, but magicked circles attracted her intense scrutiny and aid. Her power prickled at my arm hairs beneath my sleeves. The base commander's song flared in my ears. His heart was strong in drumbeats, but strain still showed through the trumpets, tubas, and flutes. The bellywood bark had saved him from death, yet he was still sorely dehydrated and enervated, as expected. He'd sleep a few hours yet as he recovered.

I offered a nod of approval to the medician.

He knelt to touch the edge of the copper circle around us. "Thank you, Lady, for extending your branches," he murmured. The heat withdrew as if inhaled. I turned to leave.

"Miss Percival? Pardon? I fear I'm almost out of bellywood bark."

I turned, frowning. "You're lead medician in the operations tent, aren't you? Go pull more out of the safe."

"There isn't any there. I already went. I thought Miss Leander might have taken it." His voice turned colder, more snide. "We thought she might have begun conducting healings in the reception tent."

Which would be a violation of our procedures, and a major snub to the medicians in operations. Miss Leander's age and experience made her the most qualified as matron, but her acute power and recklessness had also alienated her from her peers.

"She's done no healings there, nor has she pulled out the stores of bellywood. You two are the only ones with the key?"

The deep tan of his skin blanched. "Yes. If she doesn't have it, then who—"

"All the other herbs were there?"

"Yes!"

Our safe of excess herbs was kept in our personal

barracks. All medicians and nurses were on duty during the crisis. Had the barracks guards been struck down as well?

Outside, I found sick men spaced out as if in cemetery rows. All the scene required was extra dirt to pile atop them.

Captain Yancy, my escort through the night's journey, was there in the thick of things, assisting with triage. I pulled him aside and whispered my concern for the bellywood bark, and of the absence of the Sanitation Officer.

"I'll send men to your barracks, m'lady," he murmured, understanding well the need for secrecy. We could not afford a panic. "I know Officer Wagner. Played against him at Warriors. My men'll look."

It didn't surprise me that the men were acquainted through the tavern tabletop game of battling mechanical beasts. "Thank you. I also require an escort of soldiers in a few minutes, sir." He saluted acknowledgment. In the background, heavy thuds of shelling continued from the battlefield just beyond the low ridge.

I returned to the reception tent, only to find Miss Leander in an even-more-flustered state.

Instead of sorting soldiers for triage, she now sorted the living from the dead. At a glance, I knew the toll this took on her. The cacophony of illness was torture for her, but these sudden silences . . .

"With me, Miss Leander." I beckoned her outside. At this juncture, she could not break down in front of the men.

"Miss Percival, I think it's best if I stay. I could use my medician blanket here and start to heal—"

"Now, Miss Leander." I gave her a look.

She followed, her jaw in a tight line as if a bit yanked at her mouth. "All their conditions are turning to moribund at once. Please, let me call on the Lady—"

"How much bellywood do you have?"

"A half jar." With her knack for healing, that was enough for a dozen men, perhaps.

I let my eyes close for an instant. In my mind's eye, I pictured the Lady's Tree, its branches scraping the heavens. It was an image of spring verdancy and peace, even as winter still mired us in this mountain pass on the eastern side of the Pinnacles. I breathed in, wishing for a moment I could actually smell and taste the Lady's greenery on the wind, as Miss Leander professed to do.

I opened my eyes, instead knowing the squalor of bodies in rapid, foul deterioration. "You will walk with me to inspect the water tanks."

Normally, stepping away from ill men enabled Miss Leander to relax. Now there was no escape from the distorted music that tortured her ears. In the milky light of an overcast dawn, soldiers dragged themselves from their tents. Compatriots staggered together as if they'd spent the night in their cups. We walked on, surrounded by our escort of hale soldiers.

Then, as if we crossed a border, the presence of illness dissipated. Around us were healthy men, dressed for war in their green greatcoats and jodhpurs and high boots, their expressions grim. They looked as if they were girded to battle against the microscopic zymes that were laying waste to their comrades.

I realized we had indeed crossed a border—this was the other side of the camp. These men drew from a different set of water tanks.

"Miss Percival! Miss Leander!" Captain Yancy rode up to us and dismounted in a bound. He gestured his respect and leaned closer. "The safe was unlocked and is indeed devoid of bellywood. All other herbs are present."

"Our stores?" Miss Leander whispered, looking between us. "Bellywood was there yesterday. Only Marcus and I have keys. Oh Lady, the guards must be among the sick, and I didn't think—"

"A skilled hand needs no key to enter a safe, m'lady," he said.

"Sabotage." I snarled the word. "Wasters. They could have stolen everything, but instead, they toy with us. What's the word from the trenches?"

"I spoke with the Lieutenant Commander, and he says the illness has not spread through our lines, but they are wary. Whether or not the Wasters caused this, they'll take advantage."

I opened my mouth, but Miss Leander spoke first. "The sanitation stores should include chloride of lime for emergencies, if that's not stolen, too. That will be faster than boiling to sanitize water."

"I was about to say that very thing," I snapped.

"You taught me well." She looked away, somewhat chagrined.

"Indeed. Maybe next time I get a midnight missive from you requesting aid, I'll send you a note of confidence instead." I returned my focus to Captain Yancy. "What about Officer Wagner?"

"We've accounted for the rest of the sanitation division, but Wagner's not in the sick wards or his usual haunts. All guards have been alerted to look for him. We'll get him."

"*Get* him?" asked Miss Leander. "You're acting like he's guilty. He could be ill elsewhere—"

"His tent was cleared of his personal effects. Looks more like he skedaddled, m'lady. We'll search awhile more, then we may need to send for Clockwork Daggers to hunt him. The man had better hope we find him first," said Captain Yancy with a heavy sigh. Both the Caskentian army and the Queen's agents were quick to judge offenders, though Daggers were said to be far more patient in their execution techniques. "I'll see to the chloride of lime and will alert you if we find Wagner." At that, he mounted up, offered a tip of his black-brimmed hat, and took off at a canter.

Miss Leander shook her head. "Wagner's a family man with three children. He's come to me for advice on doctoring his babe with colic. All he wants is for the war to be done so he can go home. I can't believe he'd have anything to do with this sabotage, with killing so many."

I walked onward. "Those facts are the very reason why a man in Wagner's position would turn on his countrymen. Never underestimate a desperate man."

Ahead of us, three tanks towered twenty feet in height, supported by legs of stout steel as thick as a man. A pump-and-pipe system carried water from the river just beyond. Soldiers stood guard around these tanks; the tanks for the healthy side of the camp were just downriver and within view.

I looked to the commander of our guard. "The tanks must be opened and the rods withdrawn." Like the copper and wooden medician wands we carried at our sides, these tanks contained rotating spindles that the Lady had blessed within the sanctity of a circle. Water flowed through slowly enough that it was thoroughly sanitized before it reached the spigots.

It took mere minutes for the soldiers to unbolt the lid and dismantle the steam-powered motor mechanism of the spindle. The long rod was lifted out.

"It's been replaced," Miss Leander said immediately, her voice hollow. "There's no enchantment on it." Around us were mutters and gasps, the soldiers' fear shifting to anger.

I mounted the ladder to inspect the rod up close. At a glance, the sheen of water looked a lot like the glisten of magic, but I touched it and found no warmth of inlaid enchantment. I said nothing as I climbed down.

"They did maintenance two or three days ago," Miss Leander said, as I rejoined her. "Only on these tanks."

" 'They,' meaning Officer Wagner and his crew?"

She shook her head, scowling. "I still don't believe he had anything to do with this. Maybe it was one of his men."

"Which would mean that as commanding officer, he would still bear responsibility. Come along."

I sent the men at our disposal to the tanks that serviced the healthy side of the camp. Magic was evident in the sparkle on the lifted rod. The soldiers immediately reinstalled it and went on to the next, their spirits buoyed. This was good news. It meant there was an immediate source of pure water though it would quickly be exhausted by the number of needy soldiers.

"It's a symbolic attack," Miss Leander said. "The war started because of water rights."

"Their motivations aren't our worry. We needed to know the source, and now we do." I walked away and stopped. Miss Leander had stayed in place, frowning at the water tanks. A low airship thrummed overhead.

"The Wasters didn't simply remove some of the enchanted rods, or steal our herbs," she said, the latter in a whisper. "This is more. It's not dysentery, or cholera, or any of the enteric illnesses that strike a camp because of natural zymes in the water. I *know* the songs those maladies create. This is new, something different. It's intentional poison."

I nodded. Wasters were worthy of many expletives, but for a certainty, they were *not* stupid. I reached into my satchel for pen and paper. I did not trust this news to travel accurately by mouth. It took a few moments for me to write a letter to the Lieutenant Commander now in charge of Five, and another to be expedited to base camp. All water tanks, all medician storage, must be guarded.

I finished, rather pleased with myself. Miss Leander was unusually skilled, but her focus had been myopic. I had done what was required and inspected the tanks to find the problem. The crisis was not over, but we could proceed from here.

Miss Leander had wandered a short distance away to pace the embankment just behind the water tanks. Her wand and satchel smacked her hip with rhythmic beats. "There's no way to know where the water was poisoned. It could have happened in the tanks when the medician rods were removed, but the river is the ultimate source. But how far upriver? *Where?*" She stared across the water at the white slope.

"That doesn't matter if the rods function."

"But there will always be men who lazily fill their canteens from the river or go bathe—"

"In which case, they get what they deserve," I snapped. Why couldn't she let things be? "It's not as if we can put water samples in a circle and listen for zymes. We—"

A trumpet's blast echoed across the shallow valley. We froze for a split second as horror sank in, but we quickly shifted out of our paralysis. Miss Leander un-holstered her wand from its loop as I did the same with mine, the two of us relying on the weapons we had on hand.

Cantonment Five was under direct attack.

We ran through the tent-lined avenue. Around us, soldiers scampered for their duty posts—and then we crossed to the stricken side of the camp. Men unable to stand dragged themselves behind barrels and sand-bag walls, loading rifles with trembling hands. Others remained prone in snow that persisted in the shadows of the lane.

Miss Leander quite suddenly spun like a Mendal-ian dervish and threw herself to one side. I had a split second to wonder why, then the brown blur of a rider-less horse lunged from between the tents.

I had no chance to dodge. I crashed into the horse, its shoulder as solid as an iron mooring tower. My back-side met the dirt, the gray sky whirling as if viewed from a child's spin-about. Trumpets and hoofbeats and yells took on a tinny cast. I touched my head and found sticky warmth.

Then Miss Leander was over me, her hands yank-ing me up. "The blood was the horse's, not yours. You just have a concussion, thank the Lady! It'll pass by the time we reach the wards." She dragged me forward.

At that moment, I hated her, this most brilliant student of mine. For her vocal and fervent faith in the Lady, for the sensitivity that warned her of the horse's approach by the cry of its blood, for how she lorded her blessed insights over me without even intending to.

Before I found Miss Leander, I had been the most powerful medician in Caskentia. My aptitude at a young age even enabled me to have an audience before the late King Kethan. Now it was as though I wore the customary headmistress title of Miss Percival simply because I had borne the name for so long, the way one wears shabby clothes because of sentimentality and good fit.

I gritted my teeth, trying to stave off petty thoughts and the wobbling of the world. I forced my legs to run, stiff and old as they were. Pops of gunfire lit up the edge of the camp ahead. I wondered if the entire front line had fallen, or if this had been a decisive spear's point to penetrate the trenches to Five's weakest side.

No matter their goal, ours was simple: protect our patients.

We entered the outer yard of the wards. The deluge had worsened in our short time away. Ahead of me, Miss Leander balked like a horse at gallop jerked to a sudden stop. She could hear a full symphony in off-key agony.

This time, I took her by the arm. "You can still shoot." It was not a question.

She nodded. Cold as the morning was, sweat coursed meandering rivers from her temple to jaw. "It's been years, but yes. If I must." She'd likely mutter apologies all the while.

I disarmed a soldier who lay slack-jawed in a puddle of expulsions. Most men in the yard were either unconscious or too weak to assist in our defense—which was for the best, in a way. Many would have placed their guns to their own mouths rather than face capture by Wasters, who were known for their perverse brutality.

Still unsteady, I stepped as carefully as I could around bodies on the ground. Something felt wrong. I patted my hip. My medician wand was gone! That absence could be fatal amidst a zyme contamination like this. I'd need to recover it promptly.

The walls between the reception and moribund wards contained shrouded logs of dead men stacked like cordwood, five bodies high. All my years at the front, amidst this endless cycle of wars, and I had never seen the like.

"Miss Leander, Miss Percival!" called one of the soldiers, breathing hard. I recognized him as one of our escorts to the water tanks. He motioned us behind a stack of crates.

"Figure them Wasters'll head this way. They's executing any sick man they see on the ground. Easy pickings here."

"Oh Lady," murmured Miss Leander. "Mercy upon them."

As a medician, a mentor to several generations, I had never voiced my frustrations with faith. I knew undeniably of the Lady's power. I felt its wonder every day. But her mercy—that I doubted.

I checked the chambers of my gun. "Prayers later, Miss Leander. Ready yourself."

A concussive blast shuddered through the camp. More pops, nearer. I raised the Gadsden .45 in my grip, my wrist steadied by the corner of a crate.

The brown dungarees of a Waster flashed into view as the man ducked around a tent. I fired. Blood sprayed from his forearm—a mere flesh wound. A pathetic shot, courtesy of my concussion.

The soldier next to us fired his rifle. The Waster spun, a hole gaping through his chest, then flopped to earth.

Gunfire pattered close by, and far away, and all around. More bombs boomed from the ridge. We waited. Tension ached through my ready arms. Hooves clattered into the yard. "Hold! I'm looking for Miss Percival!" called a familiar voice. Captain Yancy. At least *he* still looked to me, not Miss Leander.

"Here!" I called.

He rode closer. "The Wasters are in retreat, m'lady! They had a force of their best, but we held them off. It seems they expected most of us to be sick as mutts."

"You medicians. You saved the camp, even if you can't cure us all." The raspy voice came from a soldier at our feet. Miserable as he was, he looked up with the most tender of smiles. "Miss Leander, she told us to stop eating and drinking right away. She sent away for help."

"Not fast enough. Not *enough*," said Miss Leander, voice breaking. She slipped the gun into her apron pocket, her gaze distant.

Miss Leander, Miss Leander, all praise Miss Leander. I heard it like a child's singsong taunt. Gritting my teeth, I assessed the soldiers in the yard. We needed a new plan of attack for our own battle.

I assembled the medical staff. We gathered what little bellywood bark we had for priority cases, and

I ordered the reception tent to be cleared. We had just begun the reorganization effort when the battle wounded began to stagger in.

These soldiers, we could aid. I staged men in lines at the operations tent, with Miss Leander assigned to bring the most urgent cases to the front of the queue.

As for the poisoned men, we housed them in the moribund tent. Healthy soldiers were assigned to provide them with fresh water. Those who suffered the most were dosed with morphine. All we could do was keep them hydrated and comfortable. Beyond that, they were under the Lady's care, such as it was.

At some point, the Lieutenant Commander came by. He informed me that a search was being conducted tent by tent for any Wasters or ill men, and that we had done an admirable job. It was the sort of poppycock expected to be said in public during a crisis.

The line of the injured dwindled. Poisoned men continued to die—though that, too, had slowed down. I estimated the number of dead in the thousands. A barracks had been commandeered to house the bodies.

As I made my rounds, I soon became aware that Miss Leander was missing. An orderly informed me that she had departed with a small escort.

If she had retreated to meditate on the Lady and assuage her guilt, I *planned* to be livid. Such regrets could and would come later. They always did, the way a cold draft pierces a building.

I gathered my own cadre of guards, and we traced her path back through camp. I recognized the area where I had collided with that horse, and ordered a quick search for my wand. I imagined how it must have flown from my hand at impact, and looked inside the nearest tents.

It was in the third that I found the body, and recognized the insignia. This man had not succumbed to enteric illness. I called over one of my men. "Fetch Captain Yancy immediately."

Just minutes later, the Captain arrived with his full retinue. We stood over the corpse of Sanitation Officer Wagner.

"Arsenic, no question," I said. Wagner's hands had the blue tint of oxygen deprivation, his skin shrunken by dehydration in a way not dissimilar to the other sick soldiers. Most every Caskentian camp had seen such suicide cases, often among officers. A quick search of the tent uncovered Wagner's own admission of guilt recorded in a note. He confessed he'd been paid a bag of coins by a Waster and intended to use the money to move his family south and out of Caskentia. He had thought that the contamination was meant to merely sicken men, not kill thousands.

Miss Leander needed to see this note later. She needed to know the cold truth. Perhaps it would pour some much-needed common sense into her brain.

"If he'd gone through court-martial, we would have burned him." Captain Yancy shrugged. "Now we can't even give his body to the dogs."

I nodded. "Arsenic causes unimaginable agony, but his dose was high, his symptoms brief. If he had any sort of honor, he'd have endured the same prolonged misery he wrought on his peers."

"Sir! M'lady!" called one of the privates. He stood amidst Wagner's luggage. "Is this the missing belly-wood bark?"

"Let me see!" I gasped in relief. "Oh! Rush this to the wards. It must be sanitized as a precaution. With this, we can save hundreds more men."

"Yes, m'lady!" After a nod from Captain Yancy, the soldier dashed away.

"All my men looking, and here you find Wagner, and with him the missing healing herbs." Captain Yancy gazed upon me with something akin to adoration. I couldn't say I minded. "This is something of a miracle, Miss Percival."

Miss Leander would undoubtedly credit such good fortune to the Lady. Perhaps that was true. Perhaps this *was* the Lady granting me a small measure of gratitude for doing her work. I had even recovered my wand nearby.

"I absolutely agree, Captain. Now if you'll excuse me." I had earned my miracle, but now I had a rogue medician to find.

My inquiries led me and my guards back to the water tanks, and beyond. Her group stood out like black cats against the blank hillside about a half mile away. The pickets were none too pleased that we were following the others across the pontoon bridge and up the hill. I didn't debate the foolishness of leaving the camp so soon after an attack. My escorts had their guns in hand as we trudged upward.

The snow was rendered deep gray by the afternoon shadow of the peak above. There were no trees. On this side of the Pinnacles, the bleakness of the Waste was already evident. This snow seeped into soil that could grow little more than sharp grass that made most beasts sick.

Miss Leander had set out her medician blanket. The sewn edge of the woven honeyflower stem circle glinted on the enchanted white fabric. On either side of it, she had used ground honeyflower to form smaller circles. These would likewise attract the Lady's focus for healings though these were far too small to encompass human bodies.

"Miss Leander!" I called. "What is this nonsense?"

She faced me, her fingers tangled together at her waist. "Miss Percival! If this works, maybe it will help. But I don't know. Oh Lady, I don't know."

"If what works?" I looked between the blankets and her soldiers, several of whom held metal buckets. By the strong stench, it seemed one contained vomit.

"You said earlier that water couldn't tell us if it carried poisonous zymes. Those words have itched in my brain ever since. What if I could hear poison itself?"

"You cannot because it's impossible."

She shook her head like a horse trying to slap away flies. "Nothing is impossible for the Lady. She's connected to all life, even zymes—"

"Miss Leander, do I need to repeat the fundamentals you should have learned as a child? Zymes are living beings that require a magnifying scope to be seen. We cannot hear them, only the cascading consequences they create within a body."

Avoiding my glare, Miss Leander took a bucket from a soldier. The contents sloshed. She set it in a circle on the snow, then grabbed another bucket. The soldiers looked unsettled by this confrontation between us.

"I sanitized these buckets with my wand before filling them," said Miss Leander. "One has expulsions from a sick man. One has water from the river, just downstream. These two have snow from the slope here. Guards sighted Wasters in this vicinity about three days ago, and they exchanged gunfire. It makes me wonder . . ." She set another bucket in a honeyflower circle.

"And I wonder how many men are dying because we're not in the wards," I said.

She flinched as if I'd struck her. That gave me a petty sense of satisfaction. "I must try this, Miss Percival." Her tone was soft. She knelt within her medician blanket. Snow crunched and squeaked beneath her as she folded herself into an Al Cala position.

I felt the profound urge to grab her by the arm like an unruly child, drag her back down to the camp. But no. She could look like a fool and get this charade over and done.

"Lady," she whispered. The heat of the Lady's magic

flashed against my skin. The soldiers made a collective gasp of surprise.

"We need your help, Lady. You know how these men have suffered from poison. Please, grant me your insight. Help me find the source." Her voice was muffled, her face pressed to kiss her blanket.

After a moment, she sat up, expression puckered in a frown. I turned away, ready to return to the wards. Out of the corner of my eye, I saw her stand and step across the still-activated circle. Power lapped against me. The intensity crackled like a bonfire.

Such sheer power was not normal. Not even for Miss Leander.

She stooped to touch a circle that contained another bucket. Another ripple of heat passed over me. "Please, Lady. Grace me," she said, tone reverent. An instant later, she gasped, touching her ears. "Oh, Lady. Oh my."

"What is it?" I asked, stepping closer.

"I—I hear something. Like hundreds of mice, gnawing at wood. There's a rhythm to it." Tears filled her eyes. "It's the zymes. I can hear the zymes."

"That's not possible." And yet, I knew it must be true. Deceit of this nature wasn't in her.

I had devoted my entire life to the Lady's work, to teaching her magic, her majesty. Now Miss Leander—this mere girl—had succeeded in *this*?

Miss Leander was not listening to me. She was listening to music that no medician had ever heard before. She moved from circle to circle, whispering as if in a conversation with the Lady. With her glistening white robes against gray snow, she was a figure worthy of a stained-glass window in a cathedral.

It was at that moment I realized I loathed Miss Leander.

I could have shattered that window, clawed every shard of glass from its leaden pane. Miss Leander had always been closer to the Lady than anyone I had ever known. A better healer, a more giving person. She was nice, oh so very nice, and pure and righteous. And here she had proven me wrong by simply thinking to *ask* something of the Lady.

She finished her rounds and returned to her blanket to murmur her thanks to the Lady's Tree. The circle disengaged. She looked up at me. Her expression mirrored that of the men around us, a mixture of terror and awe.

"The music of the zymes is the same in the vomit and in the river, though the vomit is far more potent. As with many zymes, they multiplied inside the body. This first pail of snow is nearly silent—we grabbed that from over there," she motioned, "But this one here, from farther down the slope, it bears the same poison. They laced it into the snow itself."

"Bloody brilliant," whispered one of the soldiers.

She nodded, clearly assuming he spoke of the Wasters and not her. "They must have tainted a large stretch of snow above the river."

"Good work, Miss Leander." I tried to place sincerity behind the words. "Your . . . eccentricity, your closeness with the Lady has likely saved many more soldiers. I'm certain the security of our sanitation efforts will be the highest priority of the command here and elsewhere."

But as I looked on her, I couldn't disguise how I felt. My hatred flushed my cheeks, constricted my throat, trembled through my fingertips. My gaze was pure, bullet-eyed envy, and I didn't care that she knew. Her throat bobbed as she swallowed and turned away. I stood taller in satisfaction. I could still make the girl quail.

"Saving the men is what matters most," she said hoarsely. "I must speak with the Lieutenant Commander, or the Colonel, if he's awake."

"*You* must speak?"

"Your pardon, Miss Percival. I'm used to being the highest-ranking medician here. That's your jurisdiction, of course."

"Yes." I paced around her, slowly, my boots crunching in the snow. "All of my medicians have toiled this day. I'll tell them this is an extraordinary discovery in the name of our academy."

"They'll know." Her words were almost indecipherable.

I stepped closer. "What was it you said, Miss Leander?"

She met my eyes. "They'll know this came from the Lady, not any of us. I was just the vessel."

My rage could not form words. I paced by her again

and again. "Since you're still laboring under the belief that you're the lead matron here, you go tell the Colonel how *your* Lady has graced you. Leave the honey-flower circles here. I will listen to the zymes as well."

We both knew I would not be able to hear the zymes, that I was her superior in title alone, but I still had to try. She collected her blanket and walked downhill with her cadre of guards.

"Miss Leander!" I called when she was about twenty feet away. She half turned toward me. "I found Officer Wagner, dead of arsenic poisoning. A suicide, complete with a note. The Wasters paid him to remove the rods. Be careful whom you trust. Your naivety might get you killed."

Grief flashed across her face. She turned away, wordless, and continued her march down the slope.

I walked around the buckets in their circles. My own blanket was in my satchel, right at my hip. I had no immediate urge to pull it out and prove my inadequacies.

"M'lady?" asked one of the men. I recognized him as the one who had made the "bloody brilliant" comment. "Would it be all right if we all had something to drink? I have these tea cans. You're welcome to one, too."

From his haversack, he pulled out slender tins of Royal-Tea, one of those newfangled commercial drinks.

"No, thank you, though it's wise of you to stay hydrated. Such tins should be safe." Empty words, advice recited from memory.

He smiled, the thick length of his mustache curving. "Do ask if you change your mind, m'lady. It's an excellent drink. Good for health!"

"Better than poisoned tank water, I'm sure." I wavered on my feet, suddenly overwhelmed by weariness, by everything. The sick men who lingered. The injured from the battle and the nearby trenches. The dead, and paperwork that came with their demise. The security of our barracks, and the water tanks, and the camp itself. All demanded immediate attention.

"She's an amazing medician, isn't she?" asked the soldier, his gaze turned to follow her downhill. "That Miss Leander?"

"Yes," I said, my voice hollow. "She's the best."

And I was not.

WINGS OF SORROW AND BONE

CHAPTER 1

The wrench wasn't Rivka's, but the heft and fit were perfect in her hand. Her tongue jabbed over her lip as she leveraged her weight through her arm. The obstinate bolt finally twisted free. She held up a small washer to her audience.

"This was the biggest problem, the one that caused so many other issues. See? One side is almost worn through."

The engineers in their coveralls stood around her, arms folded, expressions uncertain. One of the men finally held out a hand to accept the washer. With a grunt, he passed it along. "Well, I'll be. Er. Thank you, miss."

Rivka knew they had tolerated her meddling because she was an invitee to Balthazar Cody's party. His guests came from wealth and stature. They obviously weren't quite sure what to make of a young woman like her. She wasn't sure anymore, either.

The one-man band dismantled around her was the sort of advanced technology the southern nations were known for. A cylinder in the chest played tunes while the figure's sets of arms held a trumpet, chimes, flute, drum, and other instruments, all programmed to play on cue. It had created quite the impression at the party when its first song consisted of a sputtering, flatulent trumpet blast that continued a minute without ceasing. The appalled crew of engineers had hauled it down the corridor for repairs. Like a cat tempted by string, Rivka had followed.

She held up one of the articulated hands and flexed a metal pinky finger. The artistry on the construct was extraordinary, the movement almost liquid. A shame she didn't have her workbook along to sketch the schematics, but she could scribble her memories the instant she arrived home.

Across the room, a grandfather clock began to chime. She glanced up. Little airships adorned the clock's hands and hovered against a backdrop of gray-marble clouds. Nine o'clock? She had been working on the mecha for almost an hour? Beyond the carefully staged metal parts, her gloves and silk cardigan had been discarded in a wrinkled pile. Her fingertips appeared ink-dipped, her carefully done manicure ridged in black. Her dress . . .

"Damnation," she muttered. Two months of refined southern education couldn't eradicate a lifetime of Caskentian slang and blasphemy. "Grandmother is going to kill me."

Grandmother Stout regarded this as something of a societal debut for Rivka. Rivka regarded it as a form of torture that stole away time better spent on the machinery she used to pay the rent; it was important to her that she support herself as much as possible, even as she lived with Grandmother in this strange new city. Rivka had shown up on her doorstep as a refugee, a letter of introduction from Miss Leander in her hand. Days before that, Rivka hadn't known she had any living family at all. Grandmother had welcomed her wholeheartedly.

As a show of sacrifice and gratitude, Rivka even let Grandmother choose her dress for this evening. It was a ghastly, fashionable *thing*, and probably worth more than Rivka would have made in a month at the little bakery she had run in Caskentia.

She scrambled to her bare feet. The stiff leather flats hadn't proven suitable for mechanist labor best done at a squat or on her knees. Rivka touched her hopelessly stained dress and was relieved she didn't leave a new fingerprint. She gathered up her unsoiled things and shoved her feet inside her shoes.

"I wish I had time to put the automaton together again, but—"

"We can do it," a man said, his voice tight.

Conversation and the chimes of crystal echoed

down the hallway, and out of the babble she recognized Grandmother's high laugh. Rivka grimaced. Grandmother was *someone* here. She might not be as rich as many present, but she had a commanding way about her that made her seem like more. She *was* more, though very few others knew that truth.

And Rivka . . . well. She was supposed to engage in small talk and not portray any of her crude upbringing in the high towers and catwalks of neighboring Caskentia's capital of Mercia. Nor was she supposed to acknowledge reactions to her cleft lip. The polite glances, the pity, the way some people couldn't quite look at her at all. Grandmother wouldn't let Rivka wear her hair loose to hide her face, either. "Raise your chin!" Grandmother kept saying. It drove Rivka batty and made her all the more anxious to return home, to her workshop, where five projects-in-progress awaited. Dismantled engines made far better conversation companions than hoity-toity Tamarans.

Here on the fourth floor of a city tower that scraped the clouds, Mr. Cody had decorated his flat in lush gold and dark wood. The carpet was thick like storybook grass. She spied a sink through a doorway and ducked inside the chamber. Ah, hot and cold tap water—that was a luxury she had happily adjusted to here in Tamarania.

She scrubbed her hands until the oil faded to gray and tugged on gloves to cover her blackened nails. The cardigan, however, couldn't fully hide the damage to her dress. It had looked wretched on her before, and now the cloth appeared as if it had broken out in some god-awful disease.

"No point in trying to make a rabbit like you look pretty. Nothin' can hide that lip of yours." The raspy voice of Mr. Stout echoed in her brain. He'd been her benefactor, and her tormentor, when he took her in after Mama died. Rivka didn't know he was her father by blood, not until right before he'd been killed.

For a dead man, he was still terribly loud in her memory.

Rivka returned to the fringe of the party, her arms folded to hide the worst of the oil. Slipping out early wasn't an option; Grandmother had only recently dismissed extra guards from the household, certain that the threat of the Waste had abated, and she'd go loony if Rivka was out of sight too long.

If Rivka could temporarily hide from Grandmother, though, that would delay an airship's payload of nagging.

Some thirty people mingled in the parlor. Balthazar Cody was one of the augusts of the city-state of Tamarania, essentially a councilman over a city of millions. The man wielded tremendous political power, but his Arena was what made him a sensation. The next competitive bout between massive war machines would take place in a matter of weeks.

Rivka spied Grandmother; she was a pasty blot amidst the darker skin tones that dominated the room. The old woman's high mass of silver curls featured a vivid red streak that coiled into a thick bun at the back. Grandmother gesticulated punctuation to most every word in her conversation. Rivka caught her eye to offer a wave and tepid smile. Grandmother nodded acknowledgment and carried on.

Good. Rivka had been sighted. Now she could retreat again.

Cheers erupted on the other side of the room. Rivka saw the tall head of the assembled one-man band.

"You fixed it! Good-o!" called a fellow.

Rivka swallowed her annoyance. She spied a shadowed space behind two potted trees near the entry doors and stepped within the gap. Her shoulders pressed to the wall behind the trees. From here, she could monitor the room like some Clockwork Dagger engaged in espionage.

The wall quivered against her back as the doors opened to admit someone.

"Well, greetings of the evening to you!" Rivka recognized the rich tones of Balthazar Cody. The man talked like a salesman. She could barely see him through the leaves. He was likely near Grandmother's age, his skin like mahogany, his short and frizzy hair striped in white. "I wasn't sure if you'd come."

"I wasn't sure if I would, either." The voice was teenaged, maybe close to her own age. Rivka peered through the plants to see better. The girl wore a creamy column dress that contrasted with her warm, nutmeg-toned skin. Her black hair was braided and molded into triple buns. She looked like the perfect Tamaran young lady. "Why did you invite me? I doubt you've forgiven me."

Cody laughed. Guffawed, really. "You're so like your brother." He sobered. "No, I have not fully forgiven you. Because of you, I lost my grandest creation."

"I lost my brother then, too."

"Ah, your Alonzo's still alive, and I doubt he's stayed angry with you, even if you did shove his lady-love medician into a box and ship her to Mercia as freight."

Lady-love medician. They were talking about Octavia Leander. Rivka smothered her gasp with a gloved hand. Miss Leander was the kindest, strongest person Rivka had ever known—and this girl had shipped her as *freight*?

"I want to know why you invited me to your party tonight."

"You're so young to be so—"

"Why?"

"I heard your mother has fully recovered from a dreadful illness. Is it true she'll be moving here soon?"

"Yes. She's selling her house in Mercia and will move in the spring." Silence dragged out. "You want something from Mother. It's because she's in Mercia, isn't it? She knows everyone there. What, did you lose your spics during the riots?"

"Come now, I'm not permitted to care for the welfare of an old friend?"

"You've cared very little up to this point."

"Your suspicion wounds me. Consider this party invitation a gesture of reconciliation between us."

"I might as well eat. You do serve good food."

Mr. Cody laughed as he walked away.

Rivka waited a moment, then leaned out of her hiding place with a rustle of branches. "Hello! I'm Rivka Stout." The new surname still felt strange to say, but Grandmother said it was for the best, that it would raise fewer questions about their relationship. "I heard you talking to Mr. Cody. I wasn't trying to, but I was right there, and . . . anyway, you know Octavia Leander? You're Alonzo Garret's sister?"

"Oh. Yes. I'm Tatiana Garret." She quickly recovered from the surprise of someone emerging from behind potted plants. "You're related to Mrs. Stout, the publisher? Alonzo mentioned her. Why are you back there?"

"It looked cozier than anywhere else in the room." Rivka stepped out into the open again.

"What's all over your dress?"

"Just oil."

"Just oil." Tatiana arched an eyebrow. "Your accent. You're from upper Mercia, aren't you?"

Upper Mercia, meaning the towers, trams, and high catwalks. Not to be confused with the formal accent of the refined street-level denizens, with their lilting syllables and absent contractions.

"Yes. I've only been here a few months. I . . ." Rivka froze. Grandmother had worked her way through the crowd. She spoke with someone only ten feet away. If she turned, she'd see Rivka.

"Damn it. I can't stay here." She dashed toward a different hallway.

"How did you stain it like that?" Tatiana trailed her.

"The one-man band over there. I fixed it." A cheery flute carried over the conversations. Tatiana's incredulous snort made Rivka turn around with a frown. "What?"

"In the middle of Mr. Cody's party, *you* fixed a mecha."

"Why's that so hard to believe?"

"It seems very . . . Caskentian to dirty yourself like that."

"Isn't your brother from Caskentia? Aren't you?"

"I haven't lived there in years." Her tone made it clear that this was a very good thing.

They reached the end of the hallway. Rivka released a huff of breath. This didn't seem far enough from Grandmother, from everyone. As awful as Caskentia had been, as many horrible memories as she had, Rivka missed it the way a bird misses a cage. It was familiar. It was home. Defective as she was, she didn't stand out that much. Among soldiers and civilians alike, missing limbs, scars, and burns were common after fifty years of near-constant war.

Rivka tried the doorknob. It didn't budge. She stooped to stare at the lock.

"It's locked for a reason," said Tatiana. "Mr. Cody owns much of this building and the Arena next door. He doesn't want people stealing things."

"I don't intend to steal anything. I just want to get away from the party."

She pulled her small screwdriver from where she had threaded it beneath her satin belt. Grandmother was fine with her always keeping such tools on hand so long as Rivka was discreet. *"One must always be prepared!"* Grandmother often said. Considering Grandmother's own past, she'd know.

It took a matter of seconds to pick the lock; Mr. Stout's lessons had come in handy. Mr. Cody had obviously intended the mechanism to slow down rather than prevent an intruder. The high-society sorts at the party down the hall wouldn't be able to pick their own noses, much less a door.

"Then what are you doing?" asked Tatiana.

"I told you, getting away from people for a while. Why are you following me?"

"I thought we were having a conversation."

This side of the hallway looked much the same, but the feel was quite different. The sounds of the party didn't carry. Rivka released a deep breath at the welcome quiet. Seconds later, men's voices echoed down the way. Rivka and Tatiana ducked into the nearest room.

The light was dim, but Rivka could see the sheen of glass and metal. Shelves were lined with display cases of mechanical limbs. Hands, arms, legs, feet. Skin was absent, the artistry of construction bared to the eye.

"Wow," Rivka said, leaning closer to a display.

Fifty years had passed since Caskentia's Golden Age, and near-constant wars had retarded its development. Not so in the progressive southern city-states. Tamarania boasted well-kept tramways, airship buses between the metropolitan islands, even pneumatic tubes for communication within its towers.

Once Rivka was caught up with her academic work, she needed to find an apprenticeship. Tamarania abounded with masters of mechanical crafts, and Mr. Cody likely employed the best of the best. That was evident by the limbs in this room.

"My brother has a mechanical leg. I've never . . . really seen what it looks like inside." Tatiana was clearly rattled.

Rivka pulled herself away from the enrapturing displays. "I wonder what else is around here?" She looked sidelong at Tatiana. Despite her squeamishness, Tatiana didn't seem eager to go back to the party. How long had it been since Rivka had mucked about with anyone near her own age? The companionship felt . . . odd, but pleasant.

There were three more trophy rooms with limbs on display. Several other doors were locked. According to hallway signs, they contained valuable things like crystals to power mechanical limbs and silver scraps.

"Odd. The silver is locked up, but parts with integrated gold are only kept behind glass," said Rivka.

"Mr. Cody created gremlins. If any got loose inside . . ." Tatiana shrugged. "Gremlins love silver."

"Oh. I never had gremlins around. I've never even

seen one up close." Not like her part of Mercia had much silver for gremlins to steal.

The end of the hall had another locked door, this one also secured by an alarm system. Rivka couldn't resist showing off a bit since she had an audience. It took a few minutes to disarm the box. Tatiana didn't offer any praise, though. She headed straight down the hallway to where an empty lift waited.

"I've heard rumors . . ." Tatiana said as she scanned a panel labeled with the floors of the skyscraper. "There! A laboratory in the basement."

"What's down there?"

"Let's find out!" She tilted her head. "This building connects to the Arena next door. I've been in that basement with my brother. The machines down there were *marvelous*."

If they were caught deep in Mr. Cody's facility, the consequences could be much more dire than being nagged about an oil-stained dress, but Rivka was enjoying this far more than that horrid party. There was *science* to be found. She cranked the cage doors shut behind them. Tatiana managed the button panel. The lift rumbled as it descended from the fourth floor.

Rivka recalled why she wanted to speak with Tatiana in the first place. "When you were in the Arena basement, was Octavia Leander with you?"

"Yes." She scowled. "I don't like her."

"How can you not like her?" To Rivka, that sounded as plausible as hating chocolate.

"I barely get to see Alonzo. He left right away because of her." Tatiana's voice faded, then she shook herself out of it. "You heard what Mr. Cody said. I shipped Miss Leander to Mercia. I knew my mother was really sick and that Miss Leander would help. She did."

"But you still say you don't like her?"

"I used to hate her. Now . . . I don't know." Tatiana shrugged, facing away. "So how did you meet her?"

Through the gilt cage, each floor blurred by. What could Rivka really say? Miss Leander's mission in Mercia wasn't something she could talk about.

"Miss Leander changed my life," Rivka said. "I thought . . . I thought I was an orphan. I didn't know I had a grandmother or aunt or baby cousin." Or great-grandfather, though the thought of him always brought tears to Rivka's eyes. Miss Leander had recognized their familial connections through the power of her magic. "Now I live with my grandmother, Mrs. Viola Stout."

The lift came to a gentle stop. Together, they cranked open the cage doors.

Belowground, it was strangely cold. The walls were brick whitewashed in lime. She clutched her thin cardigan to her ribs. A strange sound carried from close by. Whining, crying, at various octaves. Rivka's sense of unease grew as the cacophony increased, but when Tatiana opened the next door, she didn't hesitate to walk forward.

At least a hundred cages stacked three levels high

and extended around a rectangular room of some thirty feet. Little green bodies were inside, tiny limbs flailing through the bars. The smell struck her as strange and wild, with a whiff almost like the chemical vapors of aether enchantments.

"Are those . . . gremlins?" asked Rivka.

CHAPTER 2

"Yes. Gremlins. My God, they are ugly," said Tatiana, shuddering. She had to speak loudly to be heard.

The creatures mewed, cackled, and banged on the copper and wood bars of their enclosures. Nothing was made of silver. Rivka stepped closer.

The bright electric lighting showed the green gremlins well. Some had tint variations, like patches in a quilt. Their sizes ranged from pigeon to husky tomcat. Long, bat-like wings folded along their sides. Hideous hybrid faces featured round, black eyes, some of their noses compressed and others more elongated. Their arms tended toward long and skinny, hind legs stubby.

Gremlins had split lips, just like her.

Rivka traced her upper lip with her tongue. Doctors in Tamarania could fill the gap that partially exposed her front teeth. She was slowly saving up money for that very surgery.

"Hi there." Rivka reached out. A gremlin's three small fingers clutched her fingertips. There were no claws, nor did it try to lurch her off balance. The little gremlin pressed its face to the bars. Long, whiskered ears trembled. Rivka felt a vibration against her hand, and with a start realized that the creature was purring.

"A lot of them—no, all of them—are injured." Tatiana pointed.

She was right. The gremlin whose hand Rivka held had bandages girthing most of its torso. The one to the left had no ear, just a rounded stub. The one below had no wings, and therefore, no arms. A cage over, the gremlin actually had separate arms, but its wings were gone as well.

"Is this like a medical ward for maimed gremlins?" Rivka frowned and looked around as she wiggled her hand free. It certainly seemed like a sterile surgical space. She pulled out her trusty little screwdriver again.

"What are you doing?"

"Being nosy. There has to be a ledger or something around here that chronicles their injuries."

The cages were numbered and denoted with colorful flags; not all were occupied. Most of the cabinets and drawers held tools and blades with purposes she didn't wish to contemplate. No paperwork had been left out. She pulled a cart from beneath a steel table. Lifting the hinged lid, she found a snarled pile of dead gremlins. She gasped.

"What?" called Tatiana from across the room.

"Bodies." Rivka shoved the cart away. She'd seen all kinds of dead things before, people included, but there was something especially disturbing about a haphazard knot of that nature.

Oddly enough, there had been no smell, but the handle had been warm to the touch. There must have been some kind of sanitation enchantment in place. Even so, she wiped her fingers against her skirt.

"Well, they wouldn't be able to save all of them," said Tatiana, quite matter-of-fact.

Rivka reached toward another living gremlin. A yellow flag adorned its cage along with a number fifty-three. The gremlin's little hand gripped her fingers against the bars as its mouth parted in a sound that she couldn't hear above the cacophony. She took comfort in the touch. This gremlin looked healthy, even if it lacked both wings. Maybe it wouldn't end up in that horrid cart.

Tatiana walked toward another open doorway. Rivka wiggled her fingers. The gremlin reluctantly let go.

"I'm sorry," she whispered. She felt its unblinking scrutiny as she walked around a large, steel table.

The next chamber was huge, the ceiling high. Shelves of books and storage receptacles lined the gray-brick walls. A circle of copper was inlaid in the tile floor. The copper itself was about three inches in width, flat on the floor, the circle extending some twenty feet. In the middle, thick chains were bolted to the floor and over a massive lump of dark blankets.

Blankets that moved, rising and lowering like a person slumbering.

Tatiana walked forward, her eyes wide. "This is a medician's circle. I didn't know they could be made this big."

"I thought Tamarans didn't like magic? Isn't it considered old-fashioned?" Rivka asked. "And what is *that* in the middle?"

"Most Tamarans hate magic, yes. Not Mr. Cody. He's obsessed with the subject. It's why my brother and Miss Leander ended up working with him. That thing . . . Mr. Cody *is* making a new big chimera for the Arena." Her eyes sparkled. "That's exactly what I hoped to find!"

"A big chimera for the Arena? Why?" The sport of Warriors in the Arena featured jockeyed mechanical creatures that fought for the top of a fake mountain. It was based on a tabletop game found in most taverns though those mechas were about the size of a hand. Mr. Stout had often bet on matches, big and small.

"You've been here for months. Don't you know *anything?*" Tatiana rolled her eyes. "All gremlins are chimeras. Mr. Cody originally made them from bits of other animals, but now they breed on their own. Well, a few months ago, he debuted a new creation for an Arena bout. It was part gremlin, but huge, with metal legs, arms, and wings. No one had seen the like before. My brother rode it in the Arena. He and Miss Leander named it 'Chi.' He rode away on Chi, too, when he went north."

"That's why Mr. Cody is mad at you."

"Yes, well. He'd be better off blaming Miss Leander." Tatiana stood a little straighter. "For some reason, the chimera really liked Miss Leander and Alonzo. And the Arena crowd loved the whole exhibition. Mechas in the Arena are rigged to blast fire or fly or shoot grappling hooks, all controlled by the jockey. Alonzo and the chimera worked together as an intelligent team. It was *glorious*." Her dark skin held a rosy, excited glow. "Since Mr. Cody really is making a new one, I need to talk to him again. I can be extra nice . . ."

"Talk to him about what?" asked Rivka.

Tatiana shrugged away the question as she held a hand toward the copper circle. "Feel that?"

Rivka repeated the motion. Her fingers penetrated an invisible wall that felt like hot, sticky spiderwebs. Unpleasant, certainly, but nothing like the enchantment she had crossed in Mercia with Miss Leander. Frowning to herself, Rivka walked over the copper line.

Warmth tingled across her face, as if she leaned close to a fire after being in a bitter wind. A tiny pop rang in both ears. Ahead of her, the bundle of blankets shifted, the top layer shedding onto the floor.

"What are you doing?" squealed Tatiana. "Can you even get out?"

Good grief, what *was* Rivka doing? She stuck her arm out behind her and had the same warm sensation travel over her skin.

"I'm not stuck. I think the magic is only set to contain . . . that."

"Chi killed men! Mr. Cody said so. That's why its attachment to Miss Leander and Alonzo was so strange."

"Oh. Well, this one is chained down. I don't think it can reach me." Rivka forced herself to sound nonchalant. She could easily retreat across the barrier again but remained still. The little gremlins had reacted to her with desperation and yearning. What if this creature was the same?

In the middle of the circle, the last of the blankets slithered to the floor to reveal green skin and a long, knobby ridge of spine. The beast had to be almost ten feet long. Within the constraint of chains, the body flipped with a coil of muscle. It had no extremities, only stubs where they should be. Seams and welts of stitch marks lined its skin. This creature was cobbled together with flesh, just as Mama used to mend and recreate Rivka's tattered clothes.

She sucked in a breath. "The dead gremlins. That's why their bodies are being preserved in the cart. They use them to make this big chimera."

Were the gremlins injured before they arrived in the laboratory, or were they simply there for harvest? That was the end result, certainly. Their corpses were made . . . useful in this new creation for the sake of entertainment. The sort of violent spectacle that would have delighted Mr. Stout even if he lost a month's bakery profits to his bookmaker.

The wrongness of it all caused her fists to clench at her hips.

The huge chimera's head resembled that of smaller

gremlins. Eyes were the size of round scones, black as a Waster's soul. The flesh of the brow puckered, an expression of pain. The ears looked short, unfinished. Its lips parted to reveal long teeth as it mewed like cats she had known back home, only ten times louder.

Rivka stepped closer.

"What are you doing?" hissed Tatiana.

"Look at its eyes. It's hurting." It was born of suffering, formed of creatures whose bodies lay in a naked tangle in wait of this new life.

"Are you *daft*? It's a beast for the Arena. It's supposed to tear apart machines. It can kill people."

"It can barely move. Look at these chains." Rivka approached in measured steps, a hand outstretched.

"It has teeth. It'll bite your arm off. One gulp. Or roll onto you, break all your bones—"

"Will you kindly shut up? I think the tone of your voice is bothering it."

"The tone of my . . . !"

The creature's short ears twitched as it glanced between them.

"It's okay, it's okay," Rivka murmured. "I want to check on you, that's all. Probably one of the stupidest things I've done, but it strikes me as something Octavia Leander would do. But then, she's a medician. Wait. Did you recognize her name? Do you know Miss Leander?" Each time Rivka repeated the name, the chimera's entire expression brightened.

She touched the top of the chimera's head, the broad span between its long ears. The flesh was smooth yet wrinkled, warm and lightly bristled. She gave a couple of quick strokes. The creature's expression transitioned from shock to squint-eyed bliss. An unmistakable purr rumbled through her hand.

The sound of voices carried into the chamber. Rivka turned and sprinted back through the warm veil of the circle.

"Here!" hissed Tatiana. She dragged Rivka behind a wall of crates. Behind them were shelves lined with old hardcover books and clear jars arrayed with a rainbow of herbs.

Through the gap between crates, they watched a woman enter the room. Her bountiful black hair was constrained by a massive, gold-threaded snood. Like Miss Leander, she wore the white attire of a medician, with its sparkle of cleansing enchantment, but this newcomer had considerably more style. Her robes were accented by gold trim and ruffles. The thick skirt rustled with each step.

"Get the arms ready." She motioned to unseen people. "Broderick! Get those blankets out of the circle. I told you to stop coddling the beast. It could gnaw on them and choke to death, and I daresay Mr. Cody might gnaw on *your* bones if anything were to happen at this juncture."

"I'm sorry, m'lady. I had the sense that it might be cold." A young man advanced to the edge of the circle. He wore a male version of medician gear, the narrowness of his tunic and trim white trousers revealing his lanky frame.

"Sense or not, it can endure the cold. Or learn to."

"Yes, m'lady." He raised a hand as he murmured something into the circle, then lunged forward to grab blankets by the armful. His hair, woven into a multitude of beaded dreadlocks, chimed and lashed against his shoulders. The chimera didn't move. The green body of the beast, despite its size, looked like a helpless lump in the center of the room. Its worried expression fixated on the woman in white as she opened several valises.

Men in Mr. Cody's blue livery came straight toward the crates where Rivka and Tatiana hid. The two of them retreated, following the wall around the curve of the room and farther from the door. The men opened a large box.

"Damn. I feel the magic's heat from here," muttered one.

"They been praying over these things for weeks. The legs and wings, too. Hours each day."

"Magic." One of the workers spat the word and made a slashing gesture of contempt.

"Magic, aye, but I know what I'm placing my bet on next Arena bout." The fellow jerked his head toward the circle.

Rivka was simultaneously appalled and fascinated. The research, the blueprints, the tools—she'd give anything to see what went into a project of this caliber to combine flesh and machine.

As a team, the men grunted and pulled forth a gleaming copper arm some five feet in length. They carried it into the circle and close to the chimera, then backed off quickly. The chains obviously didn't make them feel safe. The next arm was pulled out as well.

A new man entered, rolling a cart of his own. He wore a workingman's suit, his hat dangling from a pole on the cart. He offered a grunt of greeting as he set up shop beside the medician. He had to be the mechanist. Rivka had heard plenty of old soldiers talk about when their new limbs were attached, how it involved a medician and mechanist working in concert.

Her outright giddiness was held in check by the terror on the chimera's face. She desperately hoped the herbs somehow spared the chimera any pain—surely the medicians would know?

Rivka knew very little about medician magi and the Lady's Tree they worshipped. The actual Tree was located somewhere in the Waste—there had been a battle there a few months before, with Miss Leander involved—and its ancient magic connected to life all over the land. Circles like the one in the floor were used to concentrate the Lady's power, and medicians used special herbs to draw on her might to heal.

The older medician rolled up her sleeves to reveal skin hued like midnight. "Let's get this done before Cody comes down to gawk at his monster."

"Yes, Miss Arfetta," said Broderick. He wheeled in a table covered with open valises and massive herb jars. "I can likely finish the wing work afterward. There are a lot of yellow flags to tend to."

Rivka bit her fist to hold back a horrified gasp. The

little gremlin who had just clutched her hand had been designated a yellow. It must be near death, along with dozens of others. What did the other colors mean? Did she really want to know?

The circle was activated again and sent a faint wave of heat over Rivka's skin. Outside the ring, the workers waited with military posture. The medicians began to work, which involved a great deal of muttering and hand-waving and herb-sprinkling. The mechanist stared at them and every so often tweaked the mechanical arm or said something too low to hear.

It was hard to see the creature with people in the way, but they occasionally stepped aside, and Rivka could see its face.

Beady black eyes stared straight at her, unblinking. Its countenance seemed . . . blank. Braced for whatever was to come. Rivka knew that numbness. She'd known it every day for months after Mr. Stout moved her into the bakery. That constant dread of what he'd say. What he'd do. What he'd make her do.

Rivka twisted her skirt. She should speak up. She should do something. What? A hand gripped her, forced her to stay still and down. Tatiana's expression reflected dismay as she put a finger to her lips.

"This is taking forever. It's as if the Lady doesn't want to grant us help. Pah!" Miss Arfetta used a cloth to mop her brow. "At least this chimera is smaller than the first one we made. Less flesh, smaller limbs. Agility over brute strength." She stood back and nodded to herself.

"It'll need a smaller jockey then, too, won't it, m'lady?"

Beside Rivka, Tatiana fidgeted.

Miss Arfetta snorted. "Don't get any ideas, Broderick. You might be skinny as a tram rail, but you're too tall. Watch out for that jar you—" Something struck the floor with a loud ping. Her screech rose like a siren. "You clumsy oaf! You spilled pampria all over the floor! You'll need to sanitize all of it, every shred! Do you have any idea how expensive this is?"

"Yes, m'lady! I'm sorry!" He knelt and vanished from Rivka's line of sight.

"Scoop it up. Use that bag there, yes. That kind of mistake could kill someone. You know what happens when you kill a patient?"

"Yes, Miss Arfetta. You don't earn a profit."

"That's right. Now take that mess and the wand and go over there." Miss Arfetta waved. The bangles on her wrist jingled. "Make sure every last zyme is cleansed away."

"Yes, Miss Arfetta." He walked straight for their hiding place. Tatiana grabbed Rivka's arm. They couldn't retreat to the other crates, either; Mr. Cody's men still stood close by. Broderick set his things atop their crate. His white trousers showed through the gap between boxes. The sharp cinnamon-like odor of the pampria filled her senses.

Some of the red herbs spilled again, drifting between the boxes. Broderick stooped down.

His gaze met with theirs. His jaw fell slack as he emitted a yelp.

Seconds later, the other men rounded the backside of the crates. "Damn t'all!" one cried. "Where'd you gals come from?"

Tatiana stood first, arms folded over her chest. "I'm Miss Tatiana Garret, a guest of August Balthazar Cody."

Rivka felt the intense stares of the men and ducked her chin as if to hide her lip. "Me, too. A guest of Balthazar Cody, I mean. I'm Rivka Stout."

"What is this hullabaloo?" Miss Arfetta swept over, her face a dark storm cloud. "You girls, spying on us?"

"Best let Mr. Cody know," said one of the men.

"Best let me know what?" Mr. Cody's voice boomed from the entrance. "That my two youngest guests decided to explore the premises?" He glanced behind him. "Go fetch Mrs. Stout."

Tatiana curtsied as Mr. Cody approached them. Rivka followed Tatiana's example.

"It's very good to see you, Mr. Cody," said Tatiana. "This laboratory you created is a marvel!"

One of his hands rested on the great swell of his gut, which was barely restrained by a red vest. "Well, yes, but—"

"I had heard you were making another chimera, but it's amazing to actually see the process." Tatiana clutched her hands to her chest.

"I don't perform for audiences!" snapped Miss Arfetta.

"I didn't invite them down here, Miss Arfetta, I assure you." His cool gaze shifted to Rivka. "This must have been especially educational for you as an aspiring mechanist. That one-man band upstairs is playing better than when it was new. I hire the best engineers in the city, and you bested them when it came to a mere toy."

She kept her chin ducked, unsure of what to say.

"There you are, my dear!" Grandmother strolled into the room. "Goodness, the tizzy you caused! We have searched here, there, and everywhere!" She embraced Rivka, almost crushing her against the magnificent cushion of her sequined chest. Her lips pressed to Rivka's ear.

"Tell the man as little as possible. He's a rabid mouse in search of any crumb," she whispered. Grandmother turned in a dramatic gesture to beam at Tatiana. "And you are Alonzo's sister! My goodness, the resemblance! Blue eyes and all."

Tatiana curtsied again, wariness lurking behind a poised smile.

Grandmother turned her bright smile to their host. "Oh Mr. Cody, I'm so very glad for your help in finding my dear granddaughter. I hope we haven't been too much trouble. I can walk them upstairs. Tatiana, do you have an escort home?"

"One of my manservants brought me since it's after dark. I can send a message—"

"Wonderful, wonderful."

Rivka glanced at the medician's apprentice, Broderick, who stood at the back, forgotten in the fuss. He gazed at her, clearly chagrined. She gave him the tiniest of nods. They'd surprised him, so she couldn't blame him for giving them away.

Behind him, the torso of the gremlin lay very still in its circle, though it had turned just enough to keep its gaze on her. Rivka ached to hug it, even with all the risk involved, just so the chimera knew it wasn't alone. That someone cared.

She cared about the yellow-flagged little gremlins, too. What could she really do for them? The apprentice had been kind enough to give the large chimera blankets. Surely, he'd take good care of the little ones, keep them comfortable at the end.

That cart would be emptied tonight, only to be filled again.

Mr. Cody's wide grin exposed brilliant white teeth in contrast to his rich skin. Disturbing, really, how most everyone here lied through smiles all at once. "Of course they've been no trouble. They're inquisitive young ladies, dangerously bright. I hope to see you again soon, Mrs. Stout."

"I will call on you, Mr. Cody," she said airily. "Perhaps you'll need more mechanicals repaired."

Rivka turned enough to see the chimera one last time. Its brand-new arm rose, just a tad, as if to wave her farewell.

To an Arena audience, it didn't matter if mechas were destroyed in the process—they were just metal. Mr. Stout used to rejoice when word spread that jockeys were burned or crushed; he liked it when people suffered as he had.

That chimera was not metal. It knew pain. It had a soul. Rivka could tell, looking in those eyes. Same with the little ones in their cages.

Grandmother, Rivka, and Tatiana waited together for the lift. "I'm appalled, Rivka," Grandmother murmured. "Your new dress, spattered in oil!"

Rivka glanced down. "I'm sorry. I started to work, and I didn't even think about it."

"One must always think of one's attire! It's how you present yourself to the public, as important as a smile—yes, even your smile, dear child. I should note, a smile can disarm someone more readily than fisticuffs, and it will *not* destroy clothing."

"Maybe my next dress should match oil stains," Rivka muttered, feeling guilty at Grandmother's waste of money on her attire. She had to depend on Grandmother for too much already—her private tutor alone cost a fortune.

"A dress that allows spatter to blend in! Excellent idea." Grandmother nodded, not sounding the least bit facetious.

"Mrs. Stout, my brother Alonzo mentioned you when he was here," said Tatiana. "You were on that airship together?"

"*That* airship. One way of describing it though I certainly hope he granted you a more sanitized version of events."

The lift lowered into place. This time, an operator manned the station and returned them to the fourth floor. They disembarked into a quiet hallway. The doors that had been locked before were now wide open in wait for them.

"You girls make your farewells. I'll proceed to the party to fetch our hats and coats. I trust neither of you will wander again?"

The look in Grandmother's eye governed both their responses. "No, m'lady," they said, almost simultaneously. Grandmother granted them a prim, royal nod and strode down the hall.

"That was very clever, how you acted for Mr. Cody," said Rivka. "I thought we'd be boiled meat for sure."

"Like your grandmother said, a smile's a powerful thing. Mr. Cody might not be happy with us right now, but I'd much prefer to have him as an ally."

"The gremlins down there. He just creates and re-creates . . . living things? No one tries to stop him?"

"Why would they? Mr. Cody's probably one of the wealthiest men in all the city-states, and an august, too. He's not a fellow you say 'no' to. People love his Arena. They loved his first big chimera, too."

"I can't bear to think of that new one being ridden into the Arena like that. It's cruel. It's horrible." She paused, realizing how that sounded. "I'm not judging your brother for what he did before—"

"You'd better not." Tatiana's voice had an edge to it.

"Your brother was put in terrible danger by being a rider, too. That doesn't have to happen again." Rivka nodded to herself, decision made. "I need to return to Cody's laboratory."

"Why? To go into the circle again and get your head chomped off? Open up all the little cages?"

"No. Those gremlins are hurt, some of them wingless. Setting them loose in the city won't save them. It's a different sort of cruelty." So many were dead or about to die. Too many. "I need to fix this. Somehow."

That's what it came down to. Rivka couldn't tolerate it when things were broken. It made her itchy, anxious with need to get her hands into the guts of a machine and make it work. Mr. Cody seemed to do a good job of making gremlins, but assembling the big chimera . . . he was completing the job, but there was an inherent *wrongness* to it. Death was supposed to bring peace, and those little gremlins were granted no such consideration. How could a medician even be party to such a thing? Miss Leander wouldn't be. Rivka was sure of that.

"The apprentice," she said slowly. "Broderick. Maybe he would help. In any case, he'd know more about the process."

"That's an idea." Tatiana clenched Rivka's bared wrist, her fingers dark against the golden skin. "I bet I can find out where their shop is. We can ask him." For once, her smile seemed bright and genuine. "I'll call on you!" With that, Tatiana left in a swirl of skirts.

In the party, the one-man band seemed even louder, the laughter higher, the liveried servants scurrying about like ants. Like Tatiana, many of the guests wore cream-colored attire; Tamarans certainly loved their trends.

Grandmother waited by the door. She remained silent until they were farther down the hall.

"I didn't have a proper chance to nose around down there. Am I correct that Mr. Cody is in the thick of creating another of his hybrid mechanicals for the Arena?" she murmured.

"Yes." Rivka didn't feel like talking about it with Grandmother. She'd want to meddle and control.

"Hmm. Those white robes are the signature of a woman trained at Miss Percival's academy. She must have come after my time." Grandmother had no magic but had taken sanctuary at the academy through her teen years. "A medician doing that kind of insidious work. My goodness. I tell you what, Octavia Leander would be outraged. She has a peculiar fondness for gremlins."

Judging by the big chimera's reaction to Miss Leander's name, that fondness seemed to be mutual. Rivka pursed her lips in thought.

"Tatiana—Miss Garret—said she would call on me soon."

"It does my heart good to see you make a friend through mischief! Though mind you, that girl's sharp as a knife with both her wits and tongue. She cuts anyone who gets close. You know what she did to Miss Leander?" Grandmother waited for Rivka's reaction and nodded as well. "Still, I have to admire the way she handled Mr. Cody. That smile of hers could *almost* fool me. Almost."

"I don't think I'd call her a friend yet." Rivka

scarcely knew what to make of Tatiana Garret, but she was willing to help with the gremlins. That was *almost* enough.

"Whatever she is, if she's able to pry you from your gadgets for a time, bless her! Oh, I know you have excuses aplenty. You need to pay your way. You need to prove yourself. But you also need to get out! And do lift your chin when you're in society. You have nothing of which to be ashamed! Well, on *that* account. That dress of yours is a totally different matter . . ."

CHAPTER 3

Days later, Rivka and Tatiana sat together on a train headed south. Tatiana looked at ease, but Rivka could not relax. Mercia's trams were nothing like those of Tamarania. Their railcar had full-glass windows, clean floors, clean *people*. No one tried to sleep under the seats or stank of pox or tried to pickpocket or grope. The foreignness of it was disconcerting.

"That medician, Miss Arfetta, lives on the south end of the isle," said Tatiana. "It's a few more stops away."

"That far away from the plaza? What weapon do you have?" Rivka fingered the tiny screwdriver tucked into her sleeve. It'd do no good unless someone was mere inches away, but she wasn't half-bad if it came to a brawl. Her formal academics may have stopped at age nine, but Mercia had been quite educational in other ways.

Tatiana gawked. "A weapon? No one is going to bother us."

Rivka cast her a sidelong look. "Really. How often do you wander from the safety of the plaza?"

Out the window, the sky sagged with gray clouds. Raindrops dappled the glass. Airships passed every which way. Their brightly colored envelopes stood bold against the dreary backdrop. Mercia didn't have colorful airships—they were too good a target in Caskentia's constant war with the Waste.

"The south isle isn't *that* dangerous. It's not like the tenement district where most Caskentian refugees live. That's on another island altogether. This one is for . . . lower caste. Magi. Day laborers. Tamarans who get their hands dirty."

Tamarans held aether magi in good esteem, from what Rivka understood—they were necessary to run airships—but it vexed her that other magic was regarded as quaint, the very opposite of science and progress. It seemed idiotic that people couldn't appreciate magic and science together.

But then, maybe there'd be more people like Mr. Cody, too.

"How long have you lived in Tamarania?"

Tatiana continued to stare out the window, and for a minute, Rivka wondered if she had heard her. "A few years now. When Mother started to get sick, that's how she tried to hide it from me. She acted like it was all for my education, of course."

"It'll be nice for her to be here. For you to be together."

Tatiana grimaced. Rivka wondered if Tatiana's help with the gremlins was a sort of last hurrah before her freedom was greatly curtailed. Rivka could understand that, in a way. Tatiana had known years with no parents present, a life of wealth with a household of undoubtedly indulgent servants.

"It sounds like your mother was very sick. She could have died without Miss Leander's intervention." Rivka leaned closer and lowered her voice. "Trust me. Don't take her for granted. I was very close to my mama. After Papa died in the war, all we had was each other." Papa, who wasn't really her father. Her mind could never stop wrestling with that. "I was out delivering bread and making machinery repairs when our building caught fire. Mama was on the ninth floor. I watched from a neighboring tower as our tenement collapsed."

Tatiana's eyes were wide. "There were no firemen?"

"This was Mercia. The firemen came, eventually. The neighboring buildings paid to be sprayed down with water. My home . . . was mostly gone by then."

"Oh."

"It'll be a change for you to have your mother here. I know. My grandmother makes me feel like a bug beneath a boot sometimes, but I don't take her for granted. I can't."

Tatiana nodded and withdrew closer to the wall, her hands clenched on her lap.

Rivka sat back. It was strange to speak of what happened. She'd only told the full tale to Grandmother, and that had been especially hard, because of her son's role. Rivka wouldn't talk to Tatiana about *that*. Tatiana lived a different sort of life. She would never understand.

The tram squealed to a stop. Tatiana stood, and Rivka followed her to the door. Two young women in broad hats whispered to each other as they passed by.

"She looks Frengian with that light brown skin . . . sounds Caskentian."

"That lip . . . should wear a mask. Travesty here . . ."

That old, festering rage welled in Rivka's throat, and she ducked her chin, self-conscious. Soon enough, she'd have money saved up to have her lip fixed. She wouldn't need to try to hide her face anymore, or deal with these stage whispers.

She pounded out her frustration on each metal step going down, and by the time they reached street level, she was breathless yet felt better. Brick buildings around them looked old and eroded but in good shape, with windows intact and doorsteps swept. Residents reflected the same shabby tidiness, as mothers with out-of-fashion hats pushed prams loaded with babies and groceries. Older-model steam cabriolets cluttered the streets, as did numerous bicycles.

The smell struck Rivka as strange. It took her a block to realize why—there was almost no horse manure in the street, even in a poorer neighborhood such as this. The few horses they encountered were in good health, too, quite a contrast to the bony nags that dragged wagons throughout Mercia.

Rivka spied a parasol jutting out of a rubbish bun. The stick was wooden and curved. The cloth of the parasol was stained yet mostly intact, barring a few tears near the edge. She pushed the canopy open, causing Tatiana to glance back in surprise.

"What are you doing?"

"Picking up a weapon just in case. Back in Mercia, I used to carry one of Mama's old rolling pins."

"That's just a parasol," scoffed Tatiana. "And this isn't Mercia. People are *civilized* here."

Rivka pulled the parasol shut again, her grip tightening. She had imagined how her rolling pin would meet Mr. Stout's skull so many times. When Mr. Stout finally did die—though not at her hand—Rivka had been unnerved at how accurate her imagination was. The way his skull crunched. The strange, almost chemical smell it emitted.

She still dreamed of that moment. Sometimes, she wasn't sure if she'd call it a nightmare.

"A parasol can do more than ward away the sunlight and rain," she said quietly, and hooked it on her arm. "As for the civilization here, Tamarania likes to think well of itself, but there's still the Arena and that bloodlust. There's still Mr. Cody."

Tatiana dismissed the argument with a flick of her wrist. "That's still not as bad as Caskentia and its fifty years of war. You don't even see many teenaged boys there. So many are already wounded or dead."

"There are different kinds of awful." She hefted the parasol and walked on. Tatiana tried to act as nonchalant as always, but Rivka noted she was much more alert. Good.

The address Tatiana had acquired led them to a red-brick building five floors high. Beyond the roof were high spires of airship-mooring towers, some with ships attached. The wind carried a stronger scent of the sea.

They took two flights of stairs up to a cramped hallway with mostly functional electric lights. The wooden floor griped beneath every footstep. Doors were adorned with signs of various residents and businesses, ranging from homeopath to seamstress to baker. That latter made Rivka smile—a home baker, just like Mama. She inhaled deeply to take in the lovely, yeasty smell that had penetrated the corridor. Maybe as they left, she'd buy something.

Tatiana knocked on the door bearing Miss Arfetta's sign. Even her knock was clipped and commanding. The floor creaked in warning of an approach. The door cracked open.

"Miss Arfetta's Medician Shop . . . oh. It's you two." Broderick opened the door wide, his expression puzzled. "What are you doing here?"

"We're potential customers." Tatiana, short as she was, breezed inside beneath his extended arm. Rivka offered an apologetic shrug and ducked beneath his arm to follow.

They each made formal introductions. The small room sang of fragrances. Shelves lined the walls to shoulder height and displayed jars of ingredients and poultices used in common doctoring. On a table sat a large mortar and pestle, the bowl mounded with partially ground red leaves.

"Miss Arfetta is out on rounds. What did you need? I can sell you doctoring herbs, but I can't do much more, not without her present."

"We don't want to talk to her. We want to talk to you." Tatiana leaned on one hip as she gazed up at him. "We want to know more about the big gremlin."

"I'm not supposed to talk about the behemoth chimera. Trade secrets." He said it wistfully. He *wanted* to talk. Good.

"Okay then," said Rivka, her arms folded across her chest. "What do you think about the creature?" The behemoth chimera. It was good to know the proper term.

Broderick blinked. "What do I *think*?"

"Yes."

"I . . . I just . . . I do my job, but . . ."

"Miss Arfetta doesn't treat you very well," Rivka said softly.

A flush darkened his cheeks. "She's willing to apprentice me. I'm grateful for that. Most young medicians here give up, or have to go to *Caskentia* for training. But, uh. You're Caskentian, aren't you?"

Her smile was wry. "I know better than to be offended every time people shudder at the mention of my home country."

He still looked discomfited. "Sorry. It's just, Tamarania is my home. I don't want to leave if I can help it."

"Did everything go well with attaching the behemoth chimera's other arm?" Rivka asked.

He hesitated a moment, then shrugged, as if giving himself permission to talk. "Yes. The arms aren't the worst part. The legs are, and that's next. After that is the wings. The physical construction on them is about done."

"The next Arena bout is in what, three or four weeks?" asked Tatiana. "That seems awfully close."

"We started on this right after Mr. Cody lost the last chimera. The most time-consuming work is done. We made the living body, the mechanist made the limbs. We then prayed over the metal, infusing it with magic."

"Why do the arms first?" asked Rivka.

"It has to be taught how to manipulate items with hands and fingers. That fine motor work takes longer to develop than learning to walk."

Rivka recalled how it had awkwardly waved her farewell. "Don't you get tired of calling it 'it' all the time?"

"Yes, you really should name the thing. It's much tidier," said Tatiana. "Is it a girl or boy? I couldn't . . . tell."

"A behemoth gremlin doesn't have . . . outward parts. It creates vulnerability." He flushed more. "Most creatures are female by default, but Mr. Cody wanted this one more male, more aggressive."

"It didn't seem aggressive to me," said Rivka.

"Well, sure. It's chained in a circle. Get up close,

and it tries to bite. Did you see those teeth? They're made to tear through metal."

Tatiana gave Rivka a direct, appraising look.

Rivka pressed her hands together, thankful she still had them. "I say we call him Lump, because that's what he looks like."

"Not exactly the name of the next victor of the Arena," said Broderick.

"Is that what it's all about for you, making this . . . Lump into a winner?" Tatiana wrinkled her nose.

Broderick's mouth was a hard line. At midday, his jaw was already fuzzed with hair growth. "I'd rather heal people, but the behemoth chimera is Miss Arfetta's biggest contract right now. I do my job."

"And how often does she leave you here to grind herbs all day, mind the shop while she does *real* healings?"

"Tatiana?" Rivka wasn't sure why Tatiana was goading him like this, but she didn't like it.

His brown eyes turned cold. "I'm learning from Miss Arfetta."

"Certainly. Learning to use your mortar and pestle." Tatiana motioned to the work in progress on the table. "What if you could learn more? Really learn?"

"How? There are only five other master medicians in Tamarania and they already have—"

"There will be one visiting here at some point, I imagine. The best of all. She's the one who befriended that other mecha-chimera—"

"Tatiana!" snapped Rivka.

Tatiana ignored her. "See, this medician is marrying my brother, *and* she has taken over as headmistress of Miss Percival's school, so you know she's the best. Since I live here, I know they'll return eventually."

"You're talking about Miss Octavia Leander," he said slowly.

"You've heard of her?" asked Rivka.

"I suppose most all medicians have, with what she did during that poison attack during Caskentia's war last year. She's *good*." He shook his head as if dazed. "But why? What are you wanting?"

Tatiana scowled; her manipulation was too transparent. "We want to watch you work on the big chimera. Lump."

"We want to do more than watch. We want to help," added Rivka.

"Help, how?" Broderick looked between them.

"Can you get us in?" Tatiana offered a bright smile.

"Is this one of those games where we keep answering questions with questions?"

"We're not sure what we can do yet." Rivka frowned and worked her lips together as she tried to articulate her emotions into words. "But down there the other day . . . all those little gremlins, missing parts . . . seeing Lump like that, knowing he'll be sent into the Arena to maybe die . . . and the jockey would be at risk, too. Tatiana's brother was the rider in that last Arena bout. She understands the dangers involved!"

Rivka looked to her for support, but Tatiana's expression was unreadable. Maybe she couldn't bear to think of her Alonzo in such danger.

"I get it." Broderick's voice was soft. "I don't like it, either, but you two shouldn't do anything aetherbrained."

"We won't!" said Tatiana with another smile.

Broderick grunted. "I'll be there early tomorrow morning to tend the gremlins and set things up for Miss Arfetta. I can't guarantee you'll get in, but I'll see what I can do. Meet me at freight door A on the east side at nine."

"Thank you!" Tatiana almost sang. She headed toward the door while Rivka lingered by the table.

"Thank you for this. Really. I don't want to get you in trouble," she murmured.

"You won't." His tense smile said otherwise. "I don't know what you really hope to achieve, though. It's not like we can stop working on it—Lump—in the middle of the process. That's no life. Nor can you release the little gremlins. In their conditions, they have no chance in the urban wild."

She tucked down her chin and stared at her hands. "I'm a mechanist. Not certified yet or anything, but it's what I do. I fix things. I'm just not sure how to fix this yet."

She envied him, his magic. He, like Miss Leander, had a power that she could only imagine. They could save people. What could she do? By Tamaran academic standards, she was yet another ignorant Caskentian refugee. To Grandmother's dismay, Rivka's writing skills were abysmal. She had a knack for mathematics and machines, true, but had no comprehension of the advanced skills required to work on a behemoth chimera. That entailed decades of training under a true master craftsman.

"You might regret this, though," he said. "Working on the chimera won't be pretty. This is surgery, of a sort."

"I've seen blood. Death, too. That's why I don't like to see others suffer." She shrugged away images of her bloodied past. "We'll see you tomorrow."

Tatiana awaited her in the hallway, beaming like an electric light. "That went well!"

Rivka grabbed her by the arm, looming over her. "You had no right to imply Miss Leander would instruct him. You could have just asked him to help us."

"I could have, and he would have said no. What else would we do? Approach Mr. Cody directly? How do you think he'd respond? We have to get him to like us again—or even better, respect us—before we dare ask him for anything. Besides, if you've been around Miss Leander, you know she'd help him. She helps *anyone*," she said with a sneer.

Tatiana was like a feral cat Rivka once knew on a tower roof—pretty as could be, and claws quick to swipe if you got too close.

Rivka released her hold. "She helped your mother, too."

Tatiana's eyes narrowed. "Do you want to save the

gremlins or not? And Lump. What kind of name is *Lump?*"

Rivka felt so tired all of a sudden. Tired of Tatiana and her manipulations, of the sneer that crept into her voice. Tired of wondering if every whisper was about her face. She wanted to bury herself in her projects and books—even the damned grammar exercises from her tutor sounded pleasant at this point. At least she'd be home.

But the gremlins needed her. She wasn't sure how to save them, but she knew she couldn't do it alone. She didn't *want* to do it alone.

"Lump is just a name," Rivka said, looking away.

"Just a name." Tatiana harrumphed. She walked by, then turned, sudden worry crinkling her eyes. "Are you coming?"

Tatiana was scared to walk back to the tram alone. Good. She *should* be scared. Maybe on some level she knew that she couldn't bend everyone to her whim.

"Can you meet me downstairs in a few minutes?" Rivka asked as she switched the parasol hook to her other arm.

"What, are you going to talk to Broderick without me?"

Was that jealousy in Tatiana's eyes? Rivka shook her head, loose hair lashing her cheeks. "No. I'm going to buy something here. Give me a minute."

Rivka waited until she heard the stairs creak beneath Tatiana's weight, then she opened the door to the bakery. The full smell smacked her: bread, yeast, sugar, and so many childhood memories.

"Can I help you?" The woman in the kitchen had to be Grandmother's age, her skin like mahogany, her hair white and unconstrained like a halo. A table was laid out with the usual Mendalian flatbreads of the southern nations, and speckled egg rolls, and . . .

"Is that . . . a Frengian maple-sugar cake?"

"Yes, yes! Used up the last maple sugar I took as a barter. You Frengian?"

"My mama was. I'll buy a loaf." She fingered the coins in her pocket as the baker wrapped a block in paper.

As she headed downstairs, she heard heavy footsteps ascending. Tatiana's expression was anxious, angry, but upon seeing Rivka, she shifted to her usual haughtiness. "Oh. You really were buying something."

Had Tatiana really been so sure that Rivka would desert her here, without so much as a parasol for defense? Rivka paused on the steps. She broke the small loaf in half and handed over the larger piece. Food was the only way to earn the trust of feral creatures.

"Here. I don't know about you, but I'm hungry."

"What is this?" Tatiana's nose crinkled as she sniffed it.

"Maple-sugar cake. One of the best things in the world." Rivka continued downward, taking a small, delicate bite of her half. Maple-flavored glaze glossed over her tongue. The cake beneath was dense and sweet but not too sweet. Sporadic walnuts added crunch. It was perfect.

"Oh." The voice was small. "I didn't expect . . . I thought . . . Thank you."

"If you don't like it, I'll eat it. My mama used to make these." They exited the building and followed the sidewalk toward the station.

Tatiana took a bite of the cake. All was quiet but for a tram rattling overhead and the distant horn of a cabriolet. "No. It's good. I like it. Really."

They walked on together, saying a great deal through nothing at all.

CHAPTER 4

Miss Arfetta stalked before them, her boots solidly re-sounding with each step. "Those who are not graced with the powers of the Lady have difficulty understanding the miracles they witness, but I will not tolerate questions or interruptions. Nor will you gossip about what we do after the fact. I am here to work, not perform theatre. Is that understood?"

"Yes, Miss Arfetta," answered Rivka and Tatiana, almost in concert. Behind Miss Arfetta, Broderick stood at the edge of the copper circle in the laboratory. He hunkered over, not meeting their eyes. All their effort to seek out the shop on the south island, to avoid a confrontation with Mr. Cody, and Broderick broached the subject for them. Tatiana and Rivka had been met at the freight door by a cadre of Mr. Cody's guards. Mr. Cody had approved of their presence in the lab so long as they followed Miss Arfetta's rules.

Mr. Cody didn't do favors; he was like Mr. Stout in that way. Both men didn't simply like wielding power; they liked accumulating it. Mr. Cody had hoped to befriend Tatiana in order to get some connection with her mother. Now Rivka wondered what he wanted of her—or Grandmother. Her publishing company was doing very well and was probably the largest press in Tamarania that he didn't already control.

"Gentlemen!" said Miss Arfetta with a grand sweep of her arm. "Bring out the legs." The liveried men went to large crates already open on the far side of the room.

Tatiana shifted in clear discomfort.

Rivka couldn't resist sidling closer to the workmen to peer inside a box. These mechanical legs bent like the hindquarters of a horse and looked almost as tall as Rivka. The brass gleamed. The feet were broad, with three clawed toes and a rear dewclaw. She imagined it would grant a chimera more balance in the Arena, perhaps the ability to coil and jump. The massive joints certainly looked to have a lot of propulsion power.

"Back off, girl," growled a man. She glanced up. Unlike the others, this fellow wore a workingman's suit in gray, his wiry beard bushy. He glowered beneath thick, cigar-like brows.

"Oh! You're the mechanist." She kept her voice low to not attract Miss Arfetta's attention, excited as she was to meet a master craftsman. "I'd love to know what alloy—"

"Don't pretend to know what you're talking about. I don't have time for this."

That got her dander up. "I might be a woman, but—"

"What do I care for that? My daughter's my apprentice." He shook his head. "You, you're Caskentian. This job requires math, reading. I'm no schoolteacher. Leave my things be, or I'll make sure you're not in the laboratory at all."

Furious, embarrassed, she returned to Tatiana's side. She had the sudden urge to prove herself to this mechanist and was at an utter loss. She couldn't take the risk that they'd be banned from the laboratory. Helping gremlins was much more important than her pride.

Rivka looked to Lump in the middle of the circle. He was chained in place so that he lay on his right side. The topmost leg nub had been bound against his torso. A thick purple tongue draped from his mouth, his eyes shut. Broderick must have drugged him before they arrived.

What good could Rivka do here? She didn't have any magic. Like Broderick had said, this process couldn't be stopped partway. That was no life for a creature.

It took a team of about a dozen men to carry over the leg. The burly fellows were grunting and red-faced by the time they rested it on the ground to almost touch the green-fleshed body. Miss Arfetta and Broderick bustled about to ready a cart of herbs. The mechanist supervised all, arms crossed over his chest, scowl sharp as a knife's edge.

Rivka looked his way with frustration and yearning. What wonders were hidden in his tools? Did he have a model for reference? The schematics for this project? All treasures denied to her, and maybe not just for today. Would *any* mechanist in Tamarania accept her as an apprentice? Even if her lip were mended, there was still her accent, her background. If she had no place here, then where? Certainly not Caskentia.

Miss Arfetta touched the copper circle, and a wave of heat glanced over Rivka's skin even at her distance. Broderick wheeled the cart across the boundary. Miss Arfetta picked up an oversized scalpel.

"We must expose the nerve endings to attach the connector cap." Miss Arfetta turned.

Tatiana emitted a small squeak.

Broderick glanced their way, his expression apologetic. The cart and Miss Arfetta's back blocked most of their view, but Rivka couldn't miss the quiver that passed over Lump's flesh as Miss Arfetta made her first cut. Bile rose in Rivka's throat, and she stepped back.

"Don't. Go." Tatiana said it through gritted teeth.

"I can't watch them torture him. Lump felt that, did you see?"

"She's trying to drive us away. She *is* making this into theatre."

"I just . . . I . . ." Rivka had no magic. No power. No knowledge, no insight into the craft to help Lump and prevent his suffering. "I'm going to the gremlin room," she whispered, the words like gravel in her throat.

Gremlins welcomed her with mewing and flapping. She paced circles around the large table in the center of the room, anger fueling her long strides. What was she doing here? What did she really hope to achieve? Not like this room provided any respite. All those colorful flags were countdowns to doom.

She was so damned sick of feeling helpless. She hadn't been able to do anything to save Mama. If Rivka hadn't been so dense, maybe she could have prevented her death and the deaths of so many others in the tenement. Then there was Mr. Stout, those horrible months running his bakery. She couldn't leave him. She knew what became of homeless young women in Caskentia.

Her furious pace slowed. That's why she couldn't simply bury herself in work on her gadgets, as she had before the party. She looked at gremlins and saw misunderstood beings like herself.

She approached a cage, clucking her tongue to soothe them and herself. "Do you know Miss Octavia Leander?" The gremlin's long ears perked up, just as Lump's had. "Miss Leander is my friend, too. It seems like most everyone knows her."

The gremlin squawked and rubbed its face against the bars. Rivka laughed and scratched the wrinkles right between the ears. It leaned harder into her touch. The skin of this one lacked any seams. It was a born gremlin, one of the newer generation. Not that it made them any less repulsive to people.

Both its wings were gone, and judging by the bandages girthing its shoulders, it was recent. Fortunately, this one had a separate set of arms. She looked to the next cage. The gremlin there was shy, pressed against the back wall, granting her a clear view of its empty back. Both cages had red flags. Both gremlins lacked wings.

Broderick had said the wings for Lump were just about done. They'd be grafted after the metal legs.

Lump was made of the flesh of *living* animals.

Lump had such a large body, one that she could only assume had a heart, lungs, and all the body parts any person needed to survive. Hundreds, maybe thousands, of gremlins would have been required. How many more were needed? Were other animals sacrificed, too?

Lump's current pain had overwhelmed her with its cruelty, but in truth it had been multiplied beyond count.

Rivka trailed her hand along the bars. Gremlins mewed, those with hands touching her as she passed. This sordid cycle of creation needed to end. She was going to find a way, magic or not. Apprenticeship or not.

She proceeded into the laboratory. Mr. Cody had joined Tatiana.

"Well! Good to see you again, young mechanist," said Mr. Cody. His thumbs were tucked into the pockets of a red-velvet greatcoat. "Were you visiting my little gremlins?"

She sucked in a breath. That's why he let her be here. Before, he had made it clear he knew about the one-man band she fixed at his party. She had impressed him with her skills. Was that a good or bad thing?

"Yes," said Rivka. She glanced at the circle. Miss Arfetta was sprawled on the floor, her skirts edged high to reveal thick layers of lace. The mechanist stooped over her, a large wrench in hand as he twiddled with a massive mechanical knee. Broderick stood to one side, taking in everything, fidgeting with his hands at his back.

"I was just telling Mr. Cody that the latest news says three other Arena teams are starting work on behemoth chimeras. Isn't that fascinating?" Tatiana ended with a guileless smile.

"Yes, well." Mr. Cody didn't look quite as pleased. "They'll try, but so many Tamarans are leery of magic and its full potential. They want the grand results, the glorious entertainment, but they haven't spent decades on smaller chimeras as I have, or studied medician lore."

Rivka's mind raced as she took all this in. "You're saying that everything you do to gremlins, they'll do *worse*?" Tatiana rested a hand on Rivka's back, just beneath her hair.

Mr. Cody gave her a mournful nod. "Shoddy workmanship, dreadful results. Mind you, my own efforts have included plenty of failures, but as a scientist, my methods follow certain standards and procedures."

She balled her fists at her hips. "*You* have standards? What about the little gremlins? What about—" A sudden, hard tug on her hair stopped her diatribe.

Tatiana cast her an innocent smile. "Right now

I'm wondering about this chimera that's being made, and the one you had in the Arena before. Chi, I think Alonzo called it?"

"Yes. Chi." Mr. Cody shook his head in disgust.

"Chi succeeded in the Arena because of the strong bond he formed with Alonzo and Miss Leander, right?"

Rivka opened her mouth. Her hair was jerked again. What the hell was Tatiana up to? Rivka silently fumed. She didn't want to shove back or cause a scene. She had to trust that Tatiana knew what she was doing.

"Yes. I wish I hadn't lost that one so quickly. I could have learned so much." Mr. Cody shot Tatiana a withering glare; he clearly had not completely forgiven her for her role in Chi's loss. "It was a peculiar thing. Gremlins actually gossiped about Miss Leander, spoke of her as a friend. Your brother seemed to be well regarded by association."

"Spoke of her?" Rivka echoed.

"My very first gremlins have human voice boxes. Few of them are left, but they often act as translators, representatives."

Human voice boxes. Rivka felt ill.

"How do you plan to do things differently for this behemoth chimera, then?" asked Tatiana. Her hand slipped from Rivka's back. "It looks somewhat different than Chi. Lighter, maybe faster. And now maybe it'll go up against other chimera gladiatorial teams."

"Ah, you're trying to sell me something. Do go on, I like your technique."

"What are you doing?" Rivka whispered.

Tatiana kept her intent gaze on Mr. Cody. "I want to be the jockey."

"What?" Mr. Cody guffawed. "You?"

Blood rushed to Rivka's head, her fists balling at her hips. "You can't, Tatiana. That wasn't . . . you said . . ."

"I said?" Tatiana glanced at her long enough to roll her eyes.

Rivka was speechless at the betrayal. Tatiana had planned this from the start. All her hints about the laboratory and what it might contain. She had never cared about saving the gremlins. This was all about the glory of riding in the Arena.

"Miss Garret, have you piloted anything? Or driven anything, like a cabriolet or an automated cycle?"

"No. But I can do it."

"That medician, Miss Leander, put this idea in your head, didn't she? You, a jockey. Balderdash."

In the circle, Lump's torso heaved with breaths. Miss Arfetta and the mechanist continued the procedure.

"Alonzo rode your other chimera to great success. And you knew my father as an elite pilot, too," said Tatiana. "Some of the mecha pilots are my age. I'm lighter than they are."

Mr. Cody's smile was thin. "You've done some research on this subject, my dear."

Enough was enough. Rivka forced herself from numbness and took several steps away from Tatiana.

"Mr. Cody, what if you stop your experimentation once Lump's body is complete? What if he doesn't go in the Arena at all?"

Tatiana emitted a squawk of protest. Rivka silenced her with a glare.

"Pardon, but did you say 'Lump?' Did you name my wondrous chimera *Lump*?" asked Mr. Cody.

Rivka pointed to the room behind her. "Those caged gremlins are missing body parts so you can piece together your 'wondrous chimera.' They are alive and suffering. They can't fly. Some don't even have arms."

Broderick, Miss Arfetta, and all the men in the room stared.

Mr. Cody's manner shifted. "Medicians can't work with the dead. It makes it especially tricky to move internal organs. Timing and temperature must be just right. Did you know electricity can be used to restart hearts and motivate blood flow? We fuse magic and science to create something extraordinary."

"You're doing this to make a spectacle, to entertain people in the Arena. It's cruel."

"Life is cruel. Science studies the elements of life. It can't help but be cruel." Mr. Cody shook his head. "I didn't expect an urchin from Mercia to be soft as gelatin. You're like those theatre raggers from a few years ago, rallying to save horses. You don't see the big picture. My Arena bouts are important to people. They bring welcome distractions. Happiness."

Of course. Mr. Cody needed to appear as the benevolent august and distract people with his machinations. The opinion of the people was everything. It's how he stayed in office, earned his wealth.

"Mr. Cody!" Miss Arfetta strode toward the copper circle. Lump's first leg appeared to be attached to his body now. "This interruption is outrageous. We're in the midst of an operation." Her black-gloved hands were glossy. Miss Arfetta's gaze shifted to focus directly on Rivka's harelip, her own lip curled in contempt.

"Do you want this beast to suffer? To die?" Miss Arfetta asked. "It's bleeding as I talk to you. You should thank whatever you hold holy that you have no magic, that you cannot hear the suffering in its song right now."

"Then go help him!" Rivka snarled. "You're choosing to stand there. How can you call yourself a medician, make money off doing that?"

"Mr. Cody, I won't work in her presence." Miss Arfetta folded her arms and continued to stare.

Lump couldn't suffer more, not because of her. Rivka turned away. "I will go. For Lump's sake." She managed to keep her voice cool and even. Her steps were controlled and precise, her chin held high; she almost burst out in hysterical laughter at that thought. Wouldn't Grandmother be proud to see her now?

Compared to Mr. Stout, Mr. Cody and Miss Arfetta were nothing. Rivka refused to cower before them.

She bypassed the gremlin room. It was only when she was far down the hall that she began to jog as fast as her tight Tamaran skirt allowed. Her eyes burned with checked tears. She punched the buttons at the lift. Footsteps raced behind her. She tensed, ready to confront Tatiana, ready to scream and rage. Instead, it was one of Cody's men.

"I'll operate the lift, miss," he said, panting. He didn't meet her eye. She wondered if it was because of her harelip or her tears. "Where do you want to go?"

She thought of home. Her old home, before she met Miss Leander or Mr. Stout. The high towers of Mercia, with their rickety catwalks and tramways between buildings, the skyline forested with billowing smokestacks and foul gray skies. Her building, its paint peeling, furnaces cranky, the glowstone lights in the hallways so ancient that their enchantments scarcely worked at all. Her kitchen, perfumed with yeast and sugar.

"The roof. I need air," Rivka said, the words hoarse and slurred.

At the top, the cage doors opened to a brightly lit hall.

"Go left and up the stairs to the access door," he said.

Rivka barely noticed her surroundings as she followed his directions. She opened the door to find yet another stairwell. Wind nipped through the wooden slats and reminded her that she hadn't spared the time to grab her hat and coat. Birds rattled in the darkness of the eaves.

The view from the roof was far different from anything she had known in the high-rises of Mercia. Both cities had towers and compact populations, but here buildings were not quite so compressed, or stained dark by coal coke. Gray clouds thickened the sky, the faint taste of rain on the air. Four black-steel mooring towers were spaced along the roof, none of them occupied by airships.

She leaned on the icy railing. Mr. Cody lived on the famed plaza of Tamarania. The Arena was just next door—a lower, squat building with a magnificent stained-glass dome. It had mooring towers as well. A crane loaded goods onto a fat airship.

Things clattered and fluttered around her. Rivka jerked back. A gremlin—no, several gremlins—landed on the railing feet away. More sounds made her turn around. The shanty of the stairwell had a roof lined with green bodies. She hadn't heard birds in the eaves, but gremlins.

"Does Mr. Cody come here to capture your kin?" she asked, her voice choked again. "You shouldn't let him grab you. You should fight back. You don't know what he's doing." A gremlin hopped closer, its black nose twitching. "Or maybe you do," she added softly.

Rivka braced herself against the railing. Directly confronting Mr. Cody had done nothing. What would make the man realize that he wasn't simply building metal constructs like a mechanist did but living creatures? Even Tatiana intended to use Lump for her own pride and glory. Could Rivka persuade *anyone* that gremlins weren't tools to use and discard?

The wind dried tears on her cheeks, stiffened her skin. She barely flinched as a gremlin landed on her shoulder. Then another. One perched atop her head, its feet struggling for purchase in her hair. Her sob turned into a giggle.

Then, with a mad flutter, they took to the air. Rivka heard a throat clear behind her.

Broderick stood there, long and lanky in his white medician garb. "I—you don't mind if I join you?"

She turned away. "What, don't you have work to do?"

He snorted. "You saw how much actual magic I get to do. I set things up, then stand there. I happened to knock over the mechanist's wrenches just now. Miss Arfetta ordered me away, full of reminders that I'm a terrible apprentice, that I'll never be a full medician." He leaned on the railing where the gremlins had been a moment before.

"You shouldn't believe her."

"Oh, I don't, most of the time. She's a leaky gasbag, never pleased with anyone. You should see her go shopping. She makes clerks cry." He gazed out on the plaza. His hair, done in a hundred tight braids with metal beads, chimed softly beneath the wind. "I know I'm not a good medician. Not simply because of the lack of practice but because the work she does ask of me, it's . . . bad."

Rivka stilled. "She has you do the dirty work. You're the one who harvests from the gremlins and eventually kills them."

He flinched, not meeting her eye. "They're not human, but they're alive. I can hear the life in them, the way it fractures with each limb, each wing. Did you know an arm by itself in a circle still sings for a while?"

Horror silenced her. He shifted uneasily, and Rivka realized she should speak. "I didn't know that. The only medician I've been around is Miss Leander, and she was . . . different. She could hear body songs without a circle."

"I would go mad," Broderick whispered.

Rivka stared out at the city. "The color tags denote what stage the gremlins are in, right? The ones missing wings are labeled red today . . ."

"Blue means they are new and need a full examination. Green designates that's done, they are healthy, and I can proceed." His voice sounded empty. "Red notes the primary harvest is done. Yellow means I need to do a final culling. Organs and skin. If a cage has that tag, I need to finish the task as soon as possible."

Rivka tasted bile. "The gremlins in the cart were considered yellow, then?"

The gremlin who clutched her fingers the other day had been so *alive,* and she had wiggled free of its grip and abandoned it there. She had assumed the medicians knew best.

She was an idiot.

"You saw the cart?" asked Broderick. "Of course you did. Yes. It preserves them for the evening's work. Miss Arfetta wants to keep a lot of skin ready in anticipation of Arena injuries. That's going to be my major duty once Lump's attachments are done."

"Your major duty. You're going to kill *all of them*?"

"If they've contributed any parts, yes. It's more . . . merciful than releasing them. I'm trying . . . you see . . ." He took a deep breath to compose himself. "There's a group that fights against gremlin abuse. Not a very popular cause around here. I get some gremlins to them, but they don't have much money or enough space. And I can never sneak out enough of them. There are so many that . . ." He seemed to lose the ability to speak.

"I guess you expect me to ask how you can stand it since you know what you're doing is wrong." Rivka stared into her hands. Her fingers had turned ruddy with cold, but she welcomed the brisk air. "I'm not going to judge you like that. I know you hate it. I know you hate yourself."

"But I keep doing it." His laugh was choked. "I can't even figure out why. It's not even for money."

"No. It's never that straightforward. I understand that much. You're not the only one who's stained, Broderick."

She caught his steady sidelong glance. "You don't have to talk about it."

"I can. I think you'd understand more than anyone. More than Grandmother, even." Over the sprawl of the city, distant airships almost blended in with the clouds. "About the time of armistice last year, a man moved onto our tenement roof. He was badly scarred on his face and wore a mask. We all took to calling him Pigeon Man because he lived up with the birds. He came down to our flat most every day to buy bread from Mama."

Pigeon Man never said his true name. He never acted like he'd known Mama so many years before. He and Mama would have been so young back then—younger than Rivka was now. And the war had changed him. Those changes seeped far deeper than the burns across his face.

"Pigeon Man told me he wanted me to construct something for him. He had to gather the parts first. Weeks later, I was out on rounds when our building caught fire. Mama . . . hundreds of others . . ."

She drew quiet. Broderick said nothing. Even the wind slowed down to listen.

"Pigeon Man found me near the wreckage. He said he didn't think the materials would be that volatile on their own." Seeing Broderick's confusion, she continued, "I didn't know until then that what he wanted me to make was a bomb. He had stored the components on the roof."

"You didn't cause it, then. You hadn't done a thing!"

"I know that. Most of the time," she said, purposefully echoing his words. "Pigeon Man never acted sorry for what had happened. More . . . inconvenienced. Out of nowhere, he offered me a bakery to manage. He'd just won it by betting on a game of Warriors. I said yes, because it had always been Mama's dream to have a shop of her own and not work out of the flat. Besides, where else could I go?"

She couldn't say more, and not simply because of the tightness in her throat, or that the cold had shifted from being brisk to being painful. She couldn't describe the months after, her numbness, his sneers, the beatings, the horror at finding out Pigeon Man— Devin Stout—was actually her blood father.

Rivka and Broderick stared out on Tamarania City. The roundabout below was packed with steam cars and automated cycles, and few horses and wagons. Mr. Cody had said something about Rivka sounding like people who had worked to save horses. She wondered what he meant.

Miss Leander had saved Rivka from Mr. Stout. Now Rivka needed to save Lump and the other gremlins in turn. It was only right.

She looked at Broderick. "What Tatiana was saying yesterday, about Miss Leander helping with your training. I know Miss Leander, too. I think she would help you, if possible, but Tatiana can't make any guarantee. She uses people. She used me, us, from the very start so she could find some way to become a jockey." The words tasted foul in her mouth.

"I understand." Broderick slowly nodded. "I appreciate your honesty. I envy you, your strength. The way you stood up to Mr. Cody."

She said nothing. *You're not strong, rabbit. Just a weakling, ugly girl. Leave such work for men.*

"No one stands up to Miss Arfetta or Mr. Cody," continued Broderick. "You did."

"There you two are!" Tatiana's high voice rang out. Rivka spun around. Tatiana stalked toward them. "Rivka, you need to come back downstairs. That chimera—Lump—is awake and he's growling if I step near the circle—"

"Good. You shouldn't be near him, and you certainly shouldn't ride him," snapped Rivka. "That was your plan from the start, wasn't it? You never cared about saving the gremlins. It was all about your being a gallant mecha jockey like your brother."

Tatiana recoiled as if struck. "I wanted to be a jockey, yes, but I care about the gremlins. Riding on Lump is part of the grand plan to save them!"

"Then please, share this grand plan," said Rivka.

"People need to see chimeras in a different way, as something more than monsters. They only know gremlins for stealing silver and food. They can cheer for Lump!"

Broderick shook his head. "People may cheer, but they cheer for the all-metal mechanical beasts out there, too. If Lump is injured, they'll cheer even louder. It's all entertainment."

Public opinion mattered. Rivka might not be able to convince Mr. Cody and Miss Arfetta of their wrongness, but what if her voice was one of a multitude?

"How can we get people to understand that chimeras aren't really monsters?" she slowly asked.

"But they are monsters. Don't look at me like that."

Broderick held up his hands. "I'm not saying they deserve this treatment. You know I don't believe that. But behemoth chimeras are made to be both vicious and intelligent. The first big chimera killed and injured scads of men. Every time I go inside that circle these days, I wonder if I'm next."

"See, Rivka? That's why I need your help!" said Tatiana.

"Why do you say that?" Broderick asked, looking between them.

Rivka shrugged, a bit embarrassed by her own initial idiocy. "The first day we found the laboratory, I walked right up to Lump and petted him. He purred."

"Really?" His expression brightened. "No snapping, no lunging? That's curious. That doesn't mean you can let down your guard, though."

"So it's a good thing we'll have a medician with us, isn't it?" Tatiana smiled at him. He didn't smile back.

"I still don't see how riding him in the Arena will help," said Rivka.

"We'll figure that out." Tatiana flicked her wrist as she turned toward the stairs.

"No." Rivka lunged to grab her by the shoulder. "You're not going to dismiss the issue like that. This isn't about you, Tatiana. This is about Lump and the other gremlins. If you ride Lump in the Arena, we give Mr. Cody exactly what he wants. For him, it would make the deaths of the little gremlins worthwhile. Plus, it encourages more scientists to do the same awful thing."

"Wait," said Broderick, "Mr. Cody might not be the only one who gets what he wants from this. If you two really can work with Lump to get him Arena-ready, that plays into what you need, too: continued access over these next few weeks. It gives you more time."

"There's a problem with that," said Rivka. "Miss Arfetta gave me the chuck."

Tatiana grinned. "Miss Arfetta left already. Mr. Cody doesn't mind if you're in there, he said so before he departed. He thinks it'd do you good to see the mechanist's limb construction up close before the shielding skin goes over it."

Mr. Cody was setting out bait for Rivka despite all she said before. Why? What did he want from her? Could they really outmanipulate a politician of his caliber? "What if Miss Arfetta comes back?"

"If both legs are done, she won't return today," said Broderick. "She has a hair appointment this afternoon." Rivka stared at him, hoping he was being facetious. He didn't smile. "I'm the one who works down there much of the time, not her."

"See? That awful woman is gone, so come help me! Let's show Mr. Cody we can do this, and we'll figure out our plan of attack from there." Tatiana skipped toward the stairs. Rivka and Broderick followed her much more slowly.

"Damn her," Rivka growled beneath her breath. The world continued to revolve around Tatiana Garret. The noise of the gremlins faded as they entered the interior stairwell.

Broderick lingered next to Rivka. "I know you mean well," he said quietly. His words didn't echo in the passage. "But you're taking big risks here. I tranquilize the chimera if I work in close proximity. And . . . I'm not a full medician. If something happens . . ."

"If I'm stupid enough to get my arm ripped off, that's my own fault. Will Lump be in a lot of pain right now?"

"Yes. And that could make him even more aggressive." His brow furrowed. "Chimeras, even the little ones, lead hard lives. Their bodies fight against their mishmash of parts. Organ failure and tumors are common. Chimeras like Lump are so much *more* in every way, and injuries are inevitable in the Arena, too." He sighed. "Death is the only way to truly stop a chimera's pain."

CHAPTER 5

Lump stared at Rivka, one cheek scrunched against the floor. His round black eyes were lined with severe wrinkles of strain. He was still chained in place in the middle of the circle though now on his opposite side.

"Hi there," she crooned to Lump as she crept forward. His ears perked up.

She was keenly aware of how Broderick and Tatiana stared. Tension thickened the air. Rivka's hand quivered as she rubbed Lump's forehead. Sporadic whiskers poked her. It'd be so easy for him to twist around and bite her.

The purr started like a cabriolet engine. He leaned into her touch. Rivka almost sagged in relief.

"He can purr. I knew it was possible, anatomically, but . . ." Disbelief was clear in Broderick's voice.

"Silly medicians," Rivka whispered to Lump. "All

that magic, all that power, and they really don't know what they're doing, do they?"

Chains rattled as Lump lifted his head off the floor and to her knee level. Broderick yelped a warning. Rivka, stunned, didn't move back. Lump nuzzled her legs and almost bowled her over. A nervous titter escaped her lips.

"By the Lady, you're giving me a heart attack," said Broderick.

"This is your vicious behemoth chimera." Rivka rubbed Lump's head and ears. Her hand trailed around the protrusion of Lump's nose to his catlike mouth, as if she dared him to bite her. He continued to purr.

"Rivka!" Tatiana called. "Can I come over?" She waited at the copper circle.

"I think so. Approach slowly, okay?" She turned to Lump and pressed her head against his. "Tatiana is . . . well, I don't know if she's really a friend. She confuses me. But don't kill her. It would probably upset Miss Leander."

Lump chirped, the sound positive, his breath appalling.

"Where should I stand?" Tatiana stopped a few feet away, fidgeting.

"Here. Come right up next to me. Gremlins seem to sniff a lot. Don't worry. I don't think he'll bite off your arm."

"You don't *think* so? That's not very funny!" She squealed as Lump snuffled at her, his black nose leaving a moist trail down the front of her pale dress.

Rivka snorted. "You sound like an air-raid siren."

"I need to climb on Lump's back. Mr. Cody said he'd return. He needs to see that I can do this." The words were brave even as Tatiana's voice rattled like a loose turbine.

"What are you trying to prove, really?" Rivka spoke low enough so that Broderick couldn't hear from where he packed away materials.

"From the time I was young, I looked in awe at mecha pilots, but until Alonzo's match, I never considered that it was something I could do. I still wasn't sure if I could do it, then Mr. Cody laughed at me." Her gaze turned cold. "Now I *need* to."

"I wish you had a different need. I don't want either of you in the Arena."

"Then stop us before the bout happens. Stop Mr. Cody." Tatiana stated it as a challenge.

Challenge accepted. "Broderick?" Rivka called. "Can you loosen the chains?"

"I can, but if Lump rolls with her up there—"

"I won't blame you if I'm crushed to death, all right?" said Tatiana.

"Will the weight of a rider hurt Lump?" Rivka asked Broderick.

"No. His own weight is substantial. Both of you would be nothing compared to that."

"We can trust you, right?" Rivka murmured to Lump. The chimera's gaze shifted to follow Broderick. The purr stopped, replaced by an unmistakable growl. The lips bared, showing two rows of gleaming teeth. Tatiana leaped backward and to the far side of the copper line.

"Lump?" A sickening wave welled in Rivka's gut. She didn't want to lurch away, but she was keenly aware of the proximity of his mouth. It'd take a split second for her to lose an arm, or worse. She stroked his forehead again, her fingers trembling. Tense lines furrowed his green skin.

Suddenly, she understood, and realized her own stupidity. "Stop, Broderick! We can't expect him to trust you. He shouldn't trust you." The apprentice medician had torn apart gremlins to piece together Lump. His very presence meant pain and death. "Tell me how to go about adjusting the chains."

"I wish you'd get away from him," Broderick said. "This is dangerous. I don't want to be in a place where I have to heal either of you."

He didn't think he'd be able to do it.

Rivka continued to pet Lump. His hackles lowered, the growl vanishing. The purr didn't return. Lump watched Broderick with the wariness of a dog often kicked by its owner.

"Then I'll do it myself," said Rivka.

"I have the key."

"I don't need a key."

"She doesn't," added Tatiana. "That's how we managed to come down here the other day. She's good."

Rivka reached to her sleeve, where her trusty little

screwdriver was threaded. She heard a frustrated, masculine growl behind her, and the hard chime of keys hitting the tile floor.

It took Rivka a few minutes to adjust the chains. Lump was tethered at the neck and behind his front legs, with extra shackles restricting his new feet. Leather bound his arms against his torso, and Broderick slid her a knife to slit those bonds.

At last, Rivka stepped back. "Up, Lump," she called, making a rolling motion with her arms. He blinked, then imitated her gesture and rolled to his new feet for the first time. A prolonged groan escaped him.

"I'm so sorry," she whispered, and wrapped her arms around his shoulders, embracing him as well as she could. His ribs heaved as he keened in agony.

Heat crackled against Rivka's skin as the circle activated. A sudden, strange breeze caused her skirts to waft around her ankles. "Broderick, should I leave the circle so you can heal him?"

"No. Stay put. I'd never confuse your songs, and neither will the Lady. Lump is like a drum corps. You—you're wind instruments. Flutes, clarinets, a piccolo."

"Oh." That pleased her.

Broderick pulled a bag from a supply shelf. He stepped just inside the circle, sending a new warm ripple around Rivka, and threw a handful of red powder toward Lump. To Rivka's awe, it spun in the air as if dancing, bobbing until it flowed onto Lump's broad back. The red vanished. Rivka caught the wonderful scent of cinnamon.

The chimera's keening stopped though his shoulders still heaved. He pushed himself to stand, briefly stretching and testing his new legs, then squatted.

Rivka rubbed his long, tapered ears. "See, not everything Broderick does is bad."

The magic dissipated, the circle cooling in an instant. Tatiana lingered at a distance, her expression worried. She was obviously building up her courage again.

Rivka looked between Tatiana and Lump. "You know what? I'll take the risk. If he lets anyone on, it'll be me."

She flung her upper body over his back. It was wide enough that she balanced there, stiff like a plank. She hooked an arm around the far nub for a wing and dragged herself to straddle him. Her skirt hitched up and uncomfortably swaddled her thighs, exposing her petticoat and the lace of bloomers beneath.

"It's just me, Lump. I'm riding you. It's okay." He quivered, and she kept rubbing circles into his neck. Her heart thrummed like a revved engine. She'd never even been on a horse, and here she was, atop a behemoth chimera. A designer monster.

Lump's quivering stopped, and he suddenly stood erect. Rivka gripped the wing nubs as she surged upward. His body shifted from side to side as he tested the joints of his new legs.

"Tatiana, your turn." Rivka pressed down on Lump's neck. "Down," she said to him, and he lowered to squat again. He learned incredibly fast. She slid over his side to the ground and tugged her dress to proper length.

Tatiana looked terrified yet resolute. "Well, you survived. That bodes well."

Rivka snorted. "Yeah. If I'm going to kill myself in a stupid way, it'll probably involve machinery going amok."

She shushed and soothed Lump as Tatiana took her turn. Unlike Rivka, Tatiana had ridden on horses— some family friend's estate outside of Mercia, she said—and made a point of showing how to properly sit. Straight spine, relaxed seat, knees lined up just so. It also helped that her skirt was looser. Rivka let her nervously prattle on as she walked around to get a proper look at the mechanical additions.

Mr. Cody was right. This was highly relevant to her interests. She ran her hands over the smooth lines of exposed copper and brass. The soldering was almost invisible. The constructed femurs were a good ten inches across, made to support a heavy bulk. The big, clawed feet could squash a person like a bug. The knees were ball-in-socket and about the size of her head. She'd made repairs on similar limbs for automaton beasts back in Mercia.

Rivka sucked in a breath. She *could* replicate Lump's limbs on a smaller scale.

It'd take practice, some example schematics, and time to scrape up money for crystals to power each mechanism, but she could make it happen.

"I thought I was entertaining a silly whim by letting you stay. I didn't think you were fool enough to actually go near the thing."

Mr. Cody's booming voice caused Rivka to spin around. He stood in the entrance, a cadre of engineers behind him. Mr. Cody looked furious, while the other men's expressions ranged from horror to awe. Lump stiffened at Mr. Cody's words. A low growl emanated from his throat.

"Mr. Cody, sir—" started Broderick.

"Shut up," Mr. Cody snapped. "You should know very well that the chimera shouldn't even be on its feet at this point, and you're lucky that—"

"Mr. Cody, I'm the medician." Broderick's voice was level. "I listened to the chimera's song. He's able to cope with the pain for now, and I don't believe them to be in harm's way."

Mr. Cody stared at Broderick as if miniature airships had begun to fly from his mouth.

"Lump has bonded with us. He's not going to attack us," said Rivka. Though the chimera would certainly go for Mr. Cody and his men if they came within range. She knew that by the tension in his muscles and metal limbs.

"Miss Stout, that's not some pet. Miss Garret, don't move a muscle, or it may try to roll and crush you. Neither of you are Miss Leander. You don't have her incredible power. Your delusions will get you killed." He motioned to his men. "Ready tranquilizers. We need to rescue these flibbertigibbets."

Rivka thought fast. She had to show Mr. Cody that

they were in control of the situation and most certainly *not* in need of rescuing. "Lump, follow my example. Wave hello to Mr. Cody. Like this."

Lump angled his head to watch her, black eyes blinking, then mimicked her motion with his own right arm. The copper hand had three fingers, the tips featuring deep gaps where claws or other devices could be installed.

"Now do this." Rivka stomped her left foot. Lump did the same, taking care not to bring his foot too near her. The ground shuddered from his impact. A low, quiet squeak escaped from Tatiana as she clutched the wing nubs for dear life.

"Hold, men." Mr. Cody gawked at them. "You, how . . . ?"

"Let's show him a Frengian peasant dance, Lump!" Rivka said loudly, then whispered, "Tatiana, don't you dare fall off."

Rivka was a wretched dancer, but that didn't matter now. She knew the moves from Mama, sure as she knew any recipe. She angled up her arms and kicked out her right leg, as much as the skirt allowed, and pointed her toe, then did the other leg. Her knee-high boots peeked from beneath her petticoat. She didn't want to hop around and get squashed by accident, so instead she bent to one side, then the other. More kicks, these at a diagonal as she pointed the toe as if at the quarter-hour notches of a clock.

Lump's big claws scraped the stones as he struggled to lift his feet. A rumble of agony escaped him, and

Rivka felt a lurch of guilt. She bowed to each side, undulating her arms, and ended with a curtsy. Lump mirrored her, copper arm curled as if he held a skirt in his broad hand.

All was silent for a long moment. Mr. Cody and the other men stared. It was Broderick who started clapping. The others joined in, slowly, as grins crept across their faces. Mr. Cody looked downright exuberant as he stepped up to the disengaged circle. Rivka heard Lump's swift inhalation, but he didn't budge.

Mr. Cody shook his head, dazed. "How did you achieve this? From my research, I surmised that Miss Leander had some insight through her magic, but that's not possible for you."

We did this by being kind, Rivka wanted to say, but she knew that would mean nothing to Mr. Cody.

"It doesn't matter how. Look. I can ride this chimera," said Tatiana. She had her arms crossed over her chest and gripped Lump by her legs alone. Show-off.

"Your mother would have me skinned alive if I let you ride."

"I'd be even more worried about Alonzo finding out. He's much more familiar with the risks of the Arena, and he tends to be rather protective. But they don't need to know." Tatiana's grin was tight. "Keep me a secret. Just advertise that you'll have the Arena's first female jockey on your new chimera. That will get you all the publicity you want, right?"

"Yes," he said slowly. "The press would create itself. But after your mother moves here—"

"That doesn't matter yet. She won't be here until after the bout."

Tatiana and Mr. Cody stared at each other, assessing. In the quiet, chirps of gremlins carried from the far room. Lump made a loud mew, as if part of their conversation. Rivka looked between the bold brass structure of Lump's arms and legs, then to the distant doorway.

"Mr. Cody," Rivka said. "I'd like to take a few gremlins to nurse them back to health." Ones with yellow tags.

He looked taken aback. "I don't think that's a wise idea, Miss Stout. Science is brutal, as I noted before, but I don't *want* to torture them. They are disabled. Keeping them alive, coddling them, isn't necessarily kindness."

Rivka understood his viewpoint. Mr. Cody wasn't sadistic. He wasn't like Mr. Stout. But he was ignorant, and at heart, he didn't really care what happened so long as he achieved his desired results.

She thought of the women who had mumbled about her on the tram. Over the years, she'd encountered many such people who thought she should be kept housebound so others didn't have to see her face—or that she should have been smothered as a babe. Rivka knew what it meant to be regarded as disposable.

Tatiana slid over Lump's side and impacted on the ground with a grunt. "Will your grandmother let you keep gremlins?" she murmured.

That was the question, wasn't it? Grandmother

often fondly recalled how she and Miss Leander had sheltered a gremlin on their disastrous airship journey, but bringing several home was something else entirely.

"I have workshop space I call my own. I can squeeze some cages in there."

Mr. Cody snorted in a laugh. "And if they escape, they'll strip your house bare of silver and help themselves to your kitchen, like the peskiest of houseguests. Ones that can't manage a lavatory."

"You're granting permission, then?" Rivka asked.

"Perhaps. It might be educational for you to see what gremlins are really like. Tell me. How much longer will your academic studies continue?"

That was a suspiciously pointed question. "Another year or so."

He nodded, and she had a sense that he already knew her answer. "My condition for taking gremlins is this—that you consider employment here, after that year or so. I assume you intend to attach yourself to a master mechanist?"

"Yes." It was a hoarse whisper.

"I can arrange it. I collect the most talented magi and scientists in Tamarania. You've already outdone some of my best household mechanists. You can go far."

His trophy rooms. His tools. The sheer artistry of Lump.

Mr. Cody was one of the wealthiest men in Tamarania—powerful, even outside politics—and he did use that for scientific advancement. Gremlins wouldn't exist otherwise.

Yet gremlins suffered and died for his work, too.

But maybe, maybe, a powerful mechanist within his ranks could stop that. Find other methods. Her, with power, with long-term access, with machines that would bring her immeasurable joy. It would defy every awful thing Mr. Stout had ever said about her.

And yet . . . How many years would it take for Rivka to reach a level where she would hold any sway? Ten? Twenty? How many chimeras would be sacrificed as mere constructs over that span, toys for the wealthy to bang together in pitched battle?

She forced her dry throat to swallow. "Are you requiring me to sign a contract?"

His eyes gleamed. "Oh-ho! You are your grandmother's heir. No. I won't ask for a contract. You have promise, but you're young, and I daresay, you carry some foolhardy notions. It's my hope that you can mature."

So that was why he was letting her take gremlins home. He wanted the experience to sour her on their whole species.

"Well! I have another idea," said Tatiana. "I can bring them home with me instead. I have my own flat. I don't need to ask permission."

"And when your mother shows up?" Rivka muttered.

"That's weeks away." Tatiana did her dismissive wrist flick and made sure to catch Rivka's eye. Rivka had doubted Tatiana's compassion and sincerity. This act was intended to prove her conviction to the cause.

"Good luck with that." Mr. Cody chortled. "Very well. You can take three gremlins. I'll leave their cages here empty so that when you bring them back, my people will tend to them." It was quite clear what he meant by that.

Only three. Maybe there was still time to save the others. Lump's wings weren't on yet, after all.

Tatiana wore her best scowl. "I assure you, Mr. Cody, we *won't* bring them back."

CHAPTER 6

"Taking those gremlins was the stupidest idea." Tatiana threw herself down in a riveted leather chair, one hand to her forehead.

Rivka sat in a plush chair as she eyed the contents of Tatiana's flat. The decor was very white, very austere, elegant in a way that seemed devoid of personality—very Tamaran, really. She set her tool satchel by her feet.

"Your message said there was an emergency with the gremlins?"

"Yes! What am I supposed to do with them?"

Rivka shook her head. She should have known it would be an exaggeration. "Tatiana! I was in the middle of reassembling a cabriolet engine—"

"An engine? In your workshop on the tenth floor?"

"Yes, it's for the steam car of another resident. I did have some funny looks when I hauled it up in the lift the other day." Rivka made a dismissive motion and immediately realized she'd picked up the gesture from Tatiana. "I also need to complete my grammar assignment before my tutor comes later, or Grandmother will string me up like a dinner roof rat."

"Well, I have a guest bedroom that reeks of ammonia. The gremlins stripped the bed—I mean that literally! They tore the sheets into strips and wove some kind of . . . thing. It's awful! It's only been a day, and they destroyed everything in there!"

"Do you want me to take them?"

Tatiana's mouth was a tense line. "Mr. Cody knows I have the gremlins. I'll keep them here. But what purpose does this really serve?"

"Look here." Rivka opened her satchel and pulled out a book. "This isn't the best of sources since it's fairly old and only shows humans, but see?" She flipped to the first of many bookmarks. "This diagram shows how a replacement human arm is made. The skin, the metal bone, the bands for tendons . . ."

Tatiana began to fidget and frown; she simply had no stomach for the stuff.

Rivka closed the book. "I want to make replacement limbs for little gremlins and let them live full lives again."

"You gave me grief because of my idea to ride Lump in the Arena, but how is *this* supposed to help? There's a reason people cover their mechanical limbs with clothing, you know. Lump's metal extensions make him all the more monstrous."

Rivka stared at the book on her lap. "I thought it would make them look more sympathetic. See, Mr. Cody is a politician. He cares about what the people think. If we can change how citizens view gremlins, maybe they won't be so thrilled to see a mecha-chimera in the Arena. Maybe it'll be alarming rather than exciting."

"Huh." Tatiana sat back. "Now that's a good idea, but do you really think it'll be easier to change how millions of people think than to change Mr. Cody's mind?"

"Look at your dress. How everyone here must wear the same color and style." Rivka grimaced at her own dress. The waistless form was all the rage, and she had scarcely any curves to grant it shape. "Maybe we can make gremlins . . . well, fashionable." She stroked the cover of her book. "Then maybe people will care that Mr. Cody is ripping apart living gremlins to make larger ones. Broderick said all of the little ones will be killed when Lump is done. Saving these three here isn't enough."

"All of them? But there are so many!" Tatiana's eyes widened. "Constructing new extremities will be a lot harder than fixing that automaton at Mr. Cody's party."

"I know. Broderick would have to help, too. It'll also be quite expensive. I'd need crystals." That would mean digging into her savings intended for her lip surgery. Rivka could deal with that. Her lip was a cosmetic thing; giving gremlins new limbs meant something more, and this might just help save the whole room from that awful cart.

Plus, she'd rather handle the matter on her own than ask Grandmother for help. Not that she feared Grandmother would discourage her; quite the contrary. After two months in Tamarania, Rivka knew that dealing with Grandmother was like trying to harness a hurricane. She didn't want to invite that complication, or the nagging, or the reminders that Rivka should lift up her chin and be proud, et cetera.

"Then there are the schematics," Rivka continued. "Cody's designs must be secret. With only human blueprints to go by, it'll be a huge challenge. I'm starting from scratch on a different scale, and with wings, too."

Tatiana stood. "Alonzo's leg was made by a master mechanist who's supposed to be the best in Caskentia. I met him once, but I can't recall his name. I can thumb through letters to find out, then write him to see if he can help!"

"Do you—would he?" She thought back to Mr. Cody's mechanist and how he treated her. A Caskentian mechanist might refuse to help for many other reasons. "While you go through letters, I'll check on the gremlins."

Tatiana flashed her a grin and whirled away.

"Would you like an aerated water or tea first, miss?" A servant spoke up from the doorway.

Rivka hesitated. "Water would be lovely, thank you." She sounded so *proper* though she wondered if she would ever really get accustomed to being waited on.

The servant retreated. Rivka stood to fully look around the room. She gravitated toward a wooden desk stacked with texts—grammar, mathematics, biology, penmanship. A neat pile of papers contained tidy looped cursive. The sheet on top was a persuasive essay on pay raises for household staff, with arguments for and against. The subject might have been dry, but *damn*, Tatiana could write. She was as manipulative on paper as she was aloud. Rivka couldn't help but be a little jealous. As much as she loved to read, she hadn't inherited Grandmother's skill with a pen. Tatiana could sell fire to infernal magi.

"Miss?" asked the servant.

Rivka whirled around, a guilty flush heating her cheeks as she set the sheets down. "Oh, yes. Thank you." She accepted the water and took a long drink. Tiny bubbles fizzled against her upper lip. "Would you please take me to the gremlins?"

The servant led her to a shut door. "In there, miss. I recommend you duck inside and close the door fast."

Rivka did just that. Cheery squawks welcomed her, and before she could turn, they were on her. Little hands and feet scampered up her legs, surmounted her breasts, and began crazy circles around her shoulders.

"Hello to you—pfft!" She spat out a hand. "You seem happy out of your cages—gah! No fingers in my mouth, you don't need to climb my head!" She pried a hand from her ear and tried to pat her flaxen hair into place. It was bound into three braided buns in anticipation of extended hours in her workshop. Long, loose hair and fine metalwork were not a good combination.

She lowered herself to the floor and had a good look around. The mattress had been gutted, cotton fluff strewn about like a massacre. The still-curved springs had been stretched and woven with strips of blankets that created a happy riot of color. The construction was in the form of a massive teardrop, the top somehow connecting to the ceiling. A small, gremlin-sized hole was just visible on the side nearest the wall.

Meanwhile, the carpet had been untacked from the floor and bubbled up in places, as though the gremlins had burrowed beneath. Wallpaper draped in large swaths. She had a sudden sense that, given time, the gremlins could dig through the walls or ceiling. Or the sharp stink would gnaw through like acid.

She wanted to be happy that they were enjoying their newfound freedom, but as she looked around, she was at an even greater loss of how to get people to *like* gremlins and stand up against Mr. Cody. Tamarans wanted personal accomplishment, they wanted order. Gremlins were chaos swaddled in green skin.

She stroked down a gremlin's knobby spine. "I bet you could all learn to dance like Lump did yesterday, but that wouldn't win over people in the right way, either. I saw a few fellows in Mercia with trained monkeys. That's not a life you lot need. You don't need to be *used*. Mr. Cody's done enough of that."

The door pushed against her back as it opened a tad. "Rivka?" At Tatiana's voice, the gremlins scrambled for the security of their nest. The room was suddenly, strangely quiet. "I found the name! Kellar Dryn, in Leffen. I have a letter ready to go! Are you almost done in there?"

With Tatiana's writing skill, this letter of introduction might just do the trick. "Just a few more minutes."

"I'll send this to the lobby via the pneumatic. The clerk can mail it off today!" Tatiana shut the door.

Rivka clicked her tongue. A gremlin's head popped through the nest's hole, two long ears wobbling, and scampered straight to her lap. The other gremlins followed, one leaping to her shoulder, the other absolutely fascinated by the sole of her shoe.

To think, these yellow-tagged gremlins, vibrant as they were, would likely already be dead if they hadn't come home with Tatiana. She felt a lurch of grief for the ones left behind, and for Broderick.

"Be still," she said softly, tapping the one on her lap. The gremlin froze. Rivka examined it all over. The nubs at the wings had healed well. The surface area was small. That meant a lot of finesse in creating connectors so that the nerves and mechanism could work together. At some point, she'd need an aether magi to enchant the wings, too.

She released a frustrated huff. Hands and feet would be challenging in different ways due to joint articulation.

These were skills she could certainly learn under the best mechanists in Tamarania, with Mr. Cody as her sponsor. This mechanist in Caskentia—he was still Caskentian. What was a master there compared to a master here?

"I don't know how we're going to do this," she whispered. The gremlin's ears bobbed. "How to stop Mr. Cody from making more chimeras, from using you for parts, from killing the other hundred gremlins still in cages. And now other people are looking at Mr. Cody as an example as they make their own behemoth chimeras. If we let Lump go to the Arena—if we let things continue on this path—and I work for Mr. Cody, will I be able to do more good in the long run?"

"Rivka?" Tatiana rapped on the door. "You need to come out. Right now."

The gremlin hopped from her lap as she stood, but the one on her shoulder remained and mewed near her ear. She gently plucked it off and nudged the third away when it tried to latch onto her skirt.

"I'm sorry. No, *down*. I'll be back soon, I promise."

They continued to cry, but they did seem to understand the meaning of "down." That was good. She still felt the lingering tickles of their little fingers as she dove through the doorway.

She whirled around and found herself face-to-face with Grandmother. A cold anvil dropped into the pit of Rivka's stomach.

Grandmother's arms were crossed over her ruffled bosom. The swirl in her hair had been dyed into cheery streaks of blue and pink. "I believe we need to talk."

Rivka nodded and followed Grandmother into the parlor. Tatiana looked calm and collected as Grandmother passed by, but when only Rivka could see, her eyes betrayed panic. Of course—Grandmother wouldn't hesitate to write Tatiana's mother about what she was up to. The gremlins would be an issue for sure, but if Grandmother discovered Tatiana's intention to ride Lump . . .

"Imagine my surprise when I visited home to find you had again escaped the tethers of your workshop." Grandmother sat with a rustle and fluff of skirts, her hands pressed just so on her lap as she looked between Rivka and Tatiana. "It seems your mischief has continued. Now do tell me, why has Miss Garret here acquired gremlins? I could hear them. More so, I could smell them."

Rivka and Tatiana sat across from each other. Rivka stared at her lap, wondering how to even begin.

"Rivka. Child. Whatever you intend to say, raise your chin."

That caused Rivka to jerk up her head. "Do you have any idea how much I hate it when you say that?" she snapped. "I'm not a child. I'm allowed to look down sometimes. Everyone does. It doesn't always mean I'm hiding my face."

Grandmother looked taken aback. "You're right. You weren't hiding your visage just now. Something has changed."

"She stood up to Mr. Cody!" Tatiana said. "She certainly didn't have her chin down then."

"Really?" Grandmother perked up. "Do tell!"

Rivka did. She spoke of Lump, of Mr. Cody's harvest of gremlins, of Broderick's horrible labor beneath

Miss Arfetta, of how Mr. Cody's cruelty was inspiring even more cruelty. That she and Tatiana were seeking a way to save the laboratory gremlins.

Her one omission was Tatiana's intention to ride Lump in the Arena bout.

"I daresay, you two are mosquitoes setting out to cause a mighty itch! My pride is boundless!" Grandmother's eyes sparkled. "You're right that winning over the population is the surest way to scare a politician witless. Mr. Cody, Miss Arfetta, you won't change their minds. They're as dense as that Warriors' mountain in the Arena."

Rivka's fingers itched with need to do *something*. To work on diagrams, finish that engine, start on gremlin wings. She walked to the window. The view overlooked a brown-bricked building and a portion of the street below. From the fifth floor, she could barely hear the constant rumble of cabriolet wheels. The absence of horses stood out to her again.

"Grandmother, Mr. Cody said something about a campaign to save horses years ago. I've noticed very few horses on the streets here, and the ones I do see are in sound health compared to those in Caskentia. Why?"

"Oh! That. There was a play several years ago that became quite the sensation. It was told from the perspective of a drayman's horse. Started with his happy years as a colt, through various owners, abuse, love, the whole woe of a working horse's life. The original production's technical aspect was quite a marvel as well—they constructed metal horses that performers used by wires and rods, while a chorus offstage sang the lines. No one had attempted such a spectacle from a horse's perspective before. I tried to acquire the rights to publish the script in Caskentia. The government refused me a permit, said horses were too valuable to the war effort, and the play was near seditious. Bosh and tosh."

At that moment, everything fit together like moving cogs in Rivka's mind.

She whirled on her heel to face them. "That's it! *That's* how we connect with people to get to Mr. Cody. Not with a play, though. There's no time for that. We need a book written from a gremlin's perspective, showing exactly what they endure in his laboratory—"

"Yes! An exposé done in fiction. It would require some delicacy, because of potential matters of slander, but this would work!" Grandmother clasped her hands. "I could start on this tomorrow. It would require a quick deadline to be in print before the next bout—"

"Grandmother. No." Rivka grinned. "Tatiana should do it."

Tatiana looked between them. "What? Me?"

"Yes, you! You're a brilliant writer. You know the laboratory and the chimeras."

"I, well, this isn't part of the plan! Me, writing a book? I can't write a book!" Tatiana and *her* plans.

Grandmother looked only somewhat disappointed.

"Well, Miss Garret, I haven't read your work, but there is something to be said for intimacy with one's narrative. Besides, it wouldn't need to be long. Slim, pocket-sized booklets are our bestsellers here."

"Tatiana, you have a knack for being . . . persuasive. You can make people *feel* how a gremlin feels."

"You really think so? You're sure that you don't want to do this instead? The glory . . ."

Because Tatiana would certainly never pass on such an opportunity. Rivka shook her head.

Grandmother lifted a finger in a very regal gesture. "I would caution you against too much focus on glory. A work such as this, flirting with the reputation of a Tamaran august, requires a pseudonym—a pen name—and the utmost secrecy about the author's identity."

"Oh."

Rivka tried not to smile too much. Loud chattering carried from down the hall, as if the gremlins called for her. Maybe they did. "Grandmother, for the sake of Tatiana's household, do you think it's possible to train gremlins to be . . . not so pesky?"

"Ah, you are speaking of a psychological endeavor! Our little gremlin Leaf on the airship was young and bright. I say start small. Build vocabulary! Come to know the creatures. Speaking of which, gremlins can work locks, did you know? I imagine your little menagerie could wander freely whenever they so desired!" Grandmother airily waved her arm, oblivious to the sudden horror painted across Tatiana's face.

"One thing Miss Leander taught me is that there is great power in simply *asking*. Many assume they know the answer and don't bother with the question. Ask of these gremlins. Be a tutor."

Tatiana beckoned the servant. "The locks on the door. We need a bolt on the outside, something that's not silver, that can't be lifted."

The servant looked equally appalled at the idea of gremlins gallivanting about the household. "I'll send Harris shopping straightaway, miss!" She rushed away.

Tatiana straightened, calm and collected again. "Speaking of asking, Mrs. Stout, I know you write to my brother and his sweetheart. About all this . . ."

"I can imagine Mr. Garret would be disconcerted to know you had any dealings with Mr. Cody. I won't lie to him or Miss Leander, but I will not volunteer information, either. Not unless I find it necessary." Grandmother stood, with a pointed look at Rivka. "We should be getting along. I must return to my printers. Miss Garret, I will send you a note later on my expectations on this gremlins treatise. I expect my deadlines to be met!"

"I'm up to any challenge." Tatiana beckoned. "Rivka, I need to talk to you for a minute."

Grandmother headed toward the door.

Tatiana stood at the window, arms folded. "You really think I can write a book?"

"Yes. Grandmother will help. Actually, she'll probably try to help too much."

"I just . . . I wasn't sure why you let me . . ." Tatiana

shook her head, her molded hair unmoving. She looked fragile and young, and so very unlike her normal self.

Rivka shrugged. "If I can befriend a chimera that can bite off my arm, I can be friends with you."

Tatiana looked stricken for a moment, then they both burst out laughing. "I suppose if this goes well, I won't get my Arena bout." She sounded a little wistful.

"I wouldn't say that. You might not ride Lump there, but you can still be a mecha jockey someday and only put your own neck on the line. As for your mount, well, I do happen to be a mechanist in training."

Tatiana grabbed Rivka in a split-second hug, then held her at arm's length. "You know, it'll be great fun to train as a jockey for Mr. Cody, all while writing this book. He won't suspect a thing."

"I'm glad you're on *my* side," said Rivka, shaking her head. She wondered if Tatiana even knew that her brother Alonzo had been a Clockwork Dagger, one of the Queen's elite spies. Perhaps Tatiana was more like her Alonzo than she realized.

Rivka rejoined Grandmother, and together they walked down the austere white passage lined with doors. Her mind leaped ahead to the work that awaited her at home and the hope of work to come. With Grandmother's publication house putting out this book, and with Rivka already making her opinions known to Mr. Cody . . . the man would put two and two together.

He was going to assume Rivka wrote it.

That might irritate Tatiana, but it'd also keep her safer as she continued to work with him and Lump.

Meanwhile, Rivka needed to dig through her scrap bins and paperwork and start sketching metal wings as they waited for word from this mechanist in Caskentia.

"You're thinking about machines, aren't you, child? I can tell. You're gazing at invisible airships."

She fidgeted with the handle of her tool satchel. "More like invisible gremlins. I need to talk to Broderick about how a medician and mechanist work through the early stages of limb assembly. Plus, I need to see if he'll help Tatiana with details in this book."

"Mercy upon this poor boy snared in your machinations!"

"About Broderick." Rivka's brows drew together in thought. "Miss Arfetta is a terrible teacher. I know Miss Percival's academy only takes girls, but what about other medician academies for boys or men?"

"Hmm. Yes. I can make inquiries, though I didn't think you'd aim to chuck him so soon. Even I couldn't help but notice the man, and you're of age—"

"I'm not interested in him like *that*." Though she had a hunch that Tatiana was.

"Ah. You just want to use him for his magic."

"Grandmother!"

"You said as much." Grandmother pressed the button to summon a lift, her grin wicked.

"You're putting words in my mouth."

"If your emotions for him change, I want you to feel like you can speak with me. I know . . . it's hard to be a girl in your time of life, to be without a mother, to endure what you did. I had my own trials, as you know." Her voice softened, her gaze distant. "Rivka, child. I erred greatly with my son. I don't understand my own blindness of what he became. I want . . . I want to do better by you. Always know I am here."

Rivka blinked back sudden tears as she stared up at the number dial. Grandmother's plump hand slipped against hers, neither looking at each other as they waited for the lift.

CHAPTER 7

Rivka was afraid, and she coped the only way she
knew how: she built.

Blueprints sprawled across her worktable. Large
bolts and stubby pipes tamed the stubbornly curled
edges of parchment. Kellar Dryn's notes were stacked
to one side, his cramped cursive circling around
sketches and diagrams and equations. Rivka scanned
over pages as she worked with bits of metal to construct an articulated model wing. It wouldn't contain
any wiring or powering mechanisms yet. Mr. Dryn
had advised her to start with the skeleton and work
inward.

She ignored the clock and the protests of her hollow
stomach as long as she could. Finally, she wandered to
the kitchen, and with a piece of bread in her hand, she
stared out the window. Sunset smeared color down
the windows of the surrounding towers. Down in the

plaza, people would be rushing home from school and work, filling any available tram car and taxi cabriolet.

Rivka needed to go down there, terrified as she was. She needed to know if her idea was working.

She slipped on her coat and grabbed one of the freshly printed books from the shelf: *Gem: or, The True Plight of Gremlins*. Today was release day. She hugged the vivid green book to her chest, the cover bold against the deep black of her coat, and headed for the tram.

Rivka made herself read on the ride even though she had already read the novel to the point of memorization.

Gem the Gremlin was born to a first-generation gremlin chimera. He lived in a nest high above the plaza, a time of innocence and frivolity, but also of lessons. He learned to steal food or starve, that people were cruel, and that his mother was slowly dying as her body fought against cancerous lesions. Then he was captured by a man known only as The Scientist, who kept a full zoo of gremlins and other creatures that he used to piece together a behemoth chimera for use in what was simply called the Game.

Rivka looked up as she blinked back tears she couldn't contain, even after countless readings.

Advertisements for the real Arena bout plastered the gaps between windows. The event was a week away. Tatiana would be practicing with Lump right now. Rivka felt a twist of yearning. She missed Lump and the other caged gremlins. A few days ago, she and Tatiana had staged a brilliant fight in front of Mr. Cody's lackeys. Rivka had renewed her argument against the Arena match and the danger that it posed to both Tatiana and Lump. Tatiana had been pompous and utterly herself. By the time Rivka flounced away, she almost believed their own act.

The schism needed that realism. They needed Mr. Cody to believe Tatiana was blameless in the ensuing hullabaloo. If there was going to be any hullabaloo. Today would tell.

She disembarked into a teeming sea of people. It took her awhile to wade to the upper-level stairs, where she knew the vantage point would be the best.

Rivka had told Grandmother about how Mama would sell her bread on market days. If she gave someone a slice of fresh bread to sample, other passersby would notice. They would want a slice of their own, and when they enjoyed that, they sometimes purchased a full loaf to take home.

Mama always made sure to give slices to children in particular. Children had a way of making parents buy more of what they wanted.

Grandmother's inspired strategy utilized members of her publishing staff along with Broderick's gremlin-rescue peers. She deployed them with free copies of the book at major train platforms that catered to young academy and university students across Tamarania and the connected isles. Grandmother had spared no expense in her promotional efforts, especially when it became clear that Mr. Cody's female jockey was Tatiana. By that juncture, stopping Mr. Cody was an even higher priority than telling Tatiana's family of her mischief.

From Rivka's vista, she spied people carrying copies of the bright green book. Even more, people were reading it! She hugged her own book tighter against her chest.

Each free copy contained a card that stated the book could be purchased at any bookstore or found at any library within the city-states. Once the volunteers exhausted their supplies of books, they would pass out these cards as well.

It had to work. The content had to cause an outcry, and quickly. That was the only way to spare Lump from facing the mechas on Warriors' mountain, the only way to stop Broderick from his horrid duty of emptying cages in mere days.

Rivka hopped down the stairs again.

In the nearest rubbish bin, something green caught her eye. It was a copy of *Gem the Gremlin* atop the trash. She brushed it off, relieved that it looked as new as ever, then frantically lifted other papers in the receptacle to see if any other books had been discarded. What if everyone threw away their copy unread?

"This has to work," she muttered. She walked on, clutching both copies, her mind in free fall. Grandmother would be at the office. Rivka could head there now, see if she had any sales numbers yet. Surely, Grandmother would have good news.

She boarded a tram. Her thoughts tumbled together, her heart beat like a slamming piston.

"Excuse me." A young woman leaned across the seat. "Is that one of those free books?"

"Oh. Yes." Rivka turned around and faced a cover toward her.

The woman glanced at her companions. They all wore vests for a Tamaran academy. "One of our friends was given a final copy from a man out by the platform. She said what she read was good, but is the book really all about *gremlins?*" Her face twisted in disgust.

"Yes! It's a story told by the gremlin. A story based on truth. Here." Rivka held out both books to her. A young man snared the second copy.

"You already read it?" the woman asked, her eyes on the cover.

"It's short, not even a hundred pages. Reads fast, too," said Rivka. The man had already settled back in his seat, book open. "It went on sale today. You can find it at all the bookstores."

"That's where we're going right now! We have papers due soon, but . . ." The second woman's voice trailed away as she tried to read over the man's shoulder. The group huddled around both readers, their voices dropping to murmurs.

Rivka faced forward in her seat. Her empty fingers twined together, and she smiled.

Rivka and Tatiana faced each other across the shiny expanse of the Stout dining table. Tatiana leaned on her elbows, her eyes shining like stars.

"There I was, in the full jockey uniform, helmet covering my entire head so no one knew who I was. I had orders to stand behind Mr. Cody. Reporters filled the whole room. Mr. Cody started talking about how his lawyers were looking into the matter of this new book and that its dreadful Scientist might be based on him. Reporters interrupted, asking about the gremlins, about how many had died to make his new mecha-chimera, if the laboratory cages were still stocked full. It was *glorious*. Mr. Cody owns most of those papers and has controlled them for years, but they still couldn't resist such a controversy."

"How did Mr. Cody react?" asked Rivka. This was the first time she had seen Tatiana since their staged fight. So much had happened in the days since.

"He was Mr. Cody. He was smooth as pudding. He said no more gremlins were being harmed and that he was officially withdrawing Lump from the bout. Everyone started yelling. I had to turn my head away, so many bulbs flashed."

"Grandmother had a note relayed here, saying that she's been swamped by reporters, too. Her whole press is exclusively printing copies of *Gem the Gremlin* right now."

Tatiana nodded. "Lump's withdrawal from the bout is going to be the headline in all the evening papers.

You should have heard the questions yelled at Mr. Cody! He answered a few of them. He said he knew that thousands of people were offering up their homes to gremlins, and yes, he would be at the next meeting of augusts that discussed legislation on experimentation on gremlins and other beasts. But then he said he had to go, and it ended, just like that. A few reporters called out to me, too, asking if I was disappointed, if I had a statement. I just waved."

"*Are* you disappointed?" Rivka delighted in every word of the conversation, but her mind kept wandering to blueprints.

Tatiana settled back in her chair. "I'm still working with Lump every day. With you gone, I'm the only one who can safely enter his circle. And then there's the book." Her grin glowed. "I thought it would bother me that I couldn't be known as the author, but then I get to walk behind Mr. Cody and hear him damn you and your grandmother, saying he wished the Wasters had gotten you, that girls your age shouldn't be allowed to get ideas and write things like that. And *I'm standing right there*. The author. All his spies, all his intrigues, and he doesn't know."

"Grandmother says the truth is bound to come out eventually."

"It will." Tatiana looked pleased at the prospect of new fame. Rivka wondered if Tatiana would feel quite so chuffed after her mother and brother knew the full truth of it. "This big fuss will be another brief Tamaran trend, but there'll be long-term good from it, too." She stood, smoothing her bobbed hair. "I need to go see what damage those three gremlins have done to my flat today. Oh!" She patted a pocket. "Here."

She tossed a satin drawstring bag onto the table. "Mr. Cody hosted a lunch party. Whatever else can be said about the man, he does serve good food. I saw these and thought of you, so I stuffed some in my jacket pocket."

Rivka untied the bag. A sweet scent wafted over her senses as the bag fell slack to reveal a handful of shimmering maple crisps. "Why—thank you."

"Frengian maple, right? Is this something your mother used to make?"

Rivka nodded, momentarily mute. "Yes. Thank you."

"Well! I'm not sure when I'll see you next." Tatiana gave her a brief hug and practically bounded away. "But soon!"

"Yes. Soon."

She stood there for a while after the door shut. With a few crisps in her palm, she walked to the window. Maple sugar crusted the top of the small yeast crackers while the underside was caramelized and slick. The sweetness crunched between her teeth as she studied the city. In the distance, near the plaza and Mr. Cody's tower, an airship flew with a trailing small banner.

The words on the banner, in bold black print: "SAVE THE GREMLINS."

CHAPTER 8

Rain poured like viscous oil, but that didn't deter the crowds who gathered to watch the spontaneous parade. Rivka stood on a tenth-story catwalk along the plaza, Tatiana's building within sight. The metal roof overhead roared beneath the deluge, the sound like a bare-rimmed cabriolet on cobbles. Men and women pressed around her, faceless within hoods and beneath steep umbrellas, voices and rain melded in cacophony.

At the Arena below, the banners for the morrow's bout hung, sodden. A cheer rose from the throngs on the street and carried up to the people on walkways all around, from open windows, rooftops, likely even the airships circling overhead.

Then Rivka saw Lump.

He was a green-and-copper blotch as large as a lorry. Tatiana was a slender speck within the saddle cage on his back. His completed wings, webbed with living flesh, were graceful swoops stretching ten feet up, even folded. There was a bounce to his step. Maybe he reacted to the adulation of the crowd, or perhaps he also understood this jaunt was something more: that he was leaving Mr. Cody's stable. Permanently.

A nearby businessman had offered to house the behemoth chimera in his warehouse, and once spring came, there were several offers from farms to house him out in the countryside. It wasn't clear yet which option was best, but there was time, and Grandmother was nothing if not shrewd. Mr. Cody still technically owned the chimera and his associated technology, but he had ceded control.

"Mama! Mama! It's beautiful!" cried a small voice. A young child leaned against the railing, a puffy arm pointed at Lump.

The chimera vanished behind a stone building. The crowd on the walkway began to disperse. Rivka lingered as if she still saw them there on the street.

"It's beautiful." Words she wanted to glue in her mind for when she was haunted by thoughts of her own ugliness and inadequacies.

She walked toward Tatiana's flat, where Broderick, the gremlins, and an afternoon of work awaited her.

It's beautiful.

"Hold him there. Just like that," said Broderick. His eyes were closed in concentration.

He and Rivka crouched together on a medician

blanket within Tatiana's gremlin room, a gremlin between them. The blanket was a portable version of the circle like in Mr. Cody's laboratory, designed to attract the Lady's attention for healings. It was big enough for a sprawled adult though this work required them to be in close proximity. Despite Grandmother's ribbing, Rivka didn't experience any hot tingles or distracted thoughts from Broderick's closeness. He was a comfortable presence, and he seemed to feel the same.

The door to the room was wide open. The three gremlins were being housebroken. A copper cage acted as a time-out zone, where one currently moped. Grandmother had already announced a forthcoming work on the care and house-training of gremlins. Thus far, the chimeras took to their disciplinary efforts quite well. Certainly with more enthusiasm than Tatiana's beleaguered servants.

Miss Leander had written to advise that gremlins adored hard cheese, too. That reward acted as a powerful motivator.

Broderick's thumb pressed on the cauterized nub where the gremlin's wing once was. He muttered to himself, then opened his eyes as he reached for a notepad. Paragraphs of observations already littered the page. Later, he would likely rewrite his notes and mail them northward. Like Rivka, Broderick had begun an enthusiastic correspondence with Kellar Dryn as they worked together from afar to restore the gremlins.

Once spring came, Rivka and Grandmother were going to travel to Caskentia's North Country for Octavia and Alonzo's wedding. Mr. Dryn and his wife would be there as well, and he had invited them to visit his workshop afterward. Perhaps Rivka would find a place to apprentice herself after all—and in Caskentia, at that.

Rivka released the gremlin. He had a scrawny face, his ears a little high on his head, and a squeak like a wheel in need of oil. He hopped to test the edge of the circle, but the heat of the Lady's presence kept him inside.

When Broderick called on the Lady for *this* work, she answered quickly and profoundly. Her magic was like a furnace. Sweat dribbled down Rivka's back. Not that she would complain, not when she could see how Broderick's confidence—his faith—was buoyed.

He set down the pencil, the beads in his dreadlocks rustling as he lifted his head. "By the way, please thank your grandmother for me. I appreciate the invitation for tomorrow, but you know how Miss Arfetta's schedule has changed."

In *Gem*, Tatiana had written about medicians as a suffering subclass like the gremlins themselves—misunderstood by society, simply struggling to survive. People were now openly curious about the magical art, and business had boomed.

"It was only right to invite you. Tatiana can't be with us, either, of course." She grinned. "Oh, you should have seen the people outside just now, Broderick! Mr. Cody must be having conniptions."

Broderick held a cupped hand toward the gremlin.

The critter sniffed at his fingertips from several inches away. The gremlins still didn't fully trust him; Rivka needed to be present during this preparatory work.

"What will you say to Mr. Cody in his own Arena?"

"I don't know." The gremlin hopped into her lap, and she stroked the curved ridge of his spine. "I want it to be something good. Profound."

The other free gremlin loped into the room and right to the edge of the blanket. It was the sole female in the group, the boldest of the bunch. She sniffed and held an arm to the hot edge of magic, then jerked back. The one on Rivka's lap mewed and waved, as if to taunt.

The female gremlin stuck out her tongue and blew a perfect raspberry.

"That," said Broderick, laughing, "is a different sort of profound."

CHAPTER 9

"**A**re you sure he'll be here, Grandmother?"

"Absolutely! A man of his ilk, as the subject of such scrutiny, will wish to be seen on his own terms. This is his Arena, his territory. He's marked it as surely as any tomcat!"

Rivka certainly hoped not. If the Arena had any scent, it was of bodies, sweat, and the harsh lemon of cleansers, and they weren't even in the tightly pressed masses below. Grandmother had purchased a private suite not far from Cody's. The guards down the hall had been generously tipped to notify them when Mr. Cody was on the way.

Ten seats were squeezed inside the booth, arranged in two rows to overlook the Arena. The scope was . . . magnificent. Rivka hadn't expected to feel that way, knowing the horrors that could have befallen Tatiana and Lump, but the place was an architectural marvel.

The metal mountain was about a hundred feet high, with built-in switchbacks and cliffs and platforms for the mechas to claim as they battled to reach the top.

The gremlin on Rivka's shoulder chirped. It seemed only right to bring one along for this face-off with Mr. Cody. Grandmother had insisted the gremlin wear a cuff and a chain that attached to Rivka's wrist, but bold little Emerald didn't seem to mind. She was content clinging to Rivka's broad collar, her eyes wide as she took in everything.

"Anytime now." Grandmother paced, taking frequent glances at her timepiece. Two guards she'd hired lingered at the back of the suite.

Rivka smoothed her skirt. Grandmother had ordered a new dress made for this occasion, and this time Rivka had requested one of Frengian style. It was thoroughly unfashionable by Tamaran standards, with its bell sleeves, folded front, and defined and belted waist, and she loved it.

Even more, Grandmother had ordered it be dyed in a mottled gray and brown, as if it were oil-stained all over. Not that Rivka planned on fixing machinery during any fancy dinner parties anytime soon, but as Grandmother always said, one should be prepared.

Emerald the gremlin pivoted an ear, then lunged from Rivka's shoulder to the floor. Rivka followed before the chain could tighten. The guards leaped up.

"Don't go far, child!" called Grandmother, as if Rivka had any control over the matter.

Emerald scampered down the hallway. Rivka pulled on the chain with both hands, but as light as the gremlin was, she was awfully strong. Emerald hopped through a doorway, where a maid stood with a cart of fresh linens.

"Hey! You can't go in there!"

This was a suite designed for royalty. It gleamed. It had space for dozens of people to sit or lounge. A full bar stood against one wall, and by the chimes of glass, a bartender was busy in the pantry. By the location, by everything, this had to be Mr. Cody's suite. Emerald screeched and forced Rivka to turn around.

Past a buffet, a golden cage towered in the corner. Inside was a massive gremlin the size of a toddler. Rivka had never seen the like.

"You!" The maid's fingers clenched Rivka's arm.

"Let her go." One of Grandmother's men scowled from the doorway.

"Can't have just anyone in here. It's more'n my job's worth." The maid took in Rivka's odd yet luxurious dress, her focus resting on Rivka's face a bit longer than proper. Rivka stared at her evenly as she reached inside her pocket.

"For your trouble." Rivka flashed a gilly coin. "I'll only stay a few minutes."

The maid snatched the coin away. "Two minutes. The man's bound to get here anytime." She shook her head. "Gremlins as pets. Never thought I'd see the like." She stalked to her cart. The guard remained in the doorway.

Rivka walked toward the big cage. Emerald scampered up her body to claim her shoulder roost again.

On the base of the cage was a small sign: PRIME: THE FIRST GREMLIN.

"The very first gremlin? I wonder why you're still here," Rivka said. "So many of the other gremlins are getting new homes."

The construction of this gremlin was different than all the others she had seen. The wings were massive to support the body, its skin seams poorly healed and mismatched in green blotches. The snout was long, its eyes large and round like coat buttons. It looked old. Haggard.

"Been here long time." The words croaked out, and the lips parted to reveal a bitter, sharp smile. "Called personal pet for Cody."

Rivka caught her breath. "You talk." This was one of the gremlins Mr. Cody had mentioned, one that acted as translator for the rest.

"Oldest do. Also listen. We know you, what you do." Prime granted a curt nod to Emerald on her shoulder. "What you plan to do. You, like Tree Medician. To us, worth more than silver."

The Tree Medician. Miss Leander. Unable to speak through the tightness in her throat, Rivka pressed a fist to her chest to salute Prime. Then, her fingers searched her sleeve for her trusty screwdriver hidden in the seam. She leaned against the bars to work the lock.

"You need your freedom."

"Freedom?"

"You need to wait until the Arena is quiet again later tonight to leave." Hopefully no people would test the lock in the next while. "Can you do that?"

"I wait. I wait a long time." Prime's eyes stared through her. "You. More than silver."

At that, Rivka retreated from the suite. Emerald was strangely mute on her shoulder.

"Well! How far did that gremlin drag you? Did you get into mischief?" Grandmother scoured Rivka with her gaze.

"M'lady?" called one of the men. "We're being signaled. Cody's coming."

Rivka and Grandmother moved to the hallway. Mr. Cody approached with a full retinue. His stride showed no hesitation at their presence, but he did nothing to hide his grimace, as if he'd smelled a manure lorry.

"Mrs. Stout. Miss Stout," he said coolly as he bowed. "Congratulations are in order. I understand you have a bestseller across the city-states. I hope you're pleased, even as your success retards decades of scientific effort."

"Perhaps it needed to be held in check," said Rivka. "Perhaps there are things more important than innovation." She reached to stroke Emerald on her shoulder. The gremlin purred though her posture was rigid as she stared at Mr. Cody.

His gaze slid over her and the gremlin. "Miss Stout, I think you can consider any offer of future employment rescinded."

"That's fine by me. I have higher standards. Grandmother?"

"I'm ready whenever you are, child!" Grandmother advanced down the hallway, practically shoving her way through Mr. Cody's surprised retinue.

"You're not staying for the bout?" Cody called.

Rivka stepped closer to him. They were of almost equal height, Mr. Cody's stomach like a rounded barricade between them. "*This* is the bout. The chimeras won."

At that, Emerald blew a raspberry.

Rivka strode down the hall, her chin held high, gremlin purring contentment on her shoulder.

FINAL FLIGHT

I stood at the rudder wheel of my airship *Argus*, in command of a ship I did not truly control. We flew north, destination unknown. A soldier stood several feet behind me. His pistols remained holstered—he wasn't daft enough or desperate enough to fire a weapon in the control cabin of an operating airship—but he had already proven adept with his fists. My co-pilot, Ramsay, was currently getting patched up, as the sarcastic commentary he had offered was not kindly received.

Throughout the cabin, tension prickled beneath the surface like an invisible rash we couldn't scratch. Everyone stood or sat rigid at their posts, gazes flickering between their gauges, the windows, and the soldiers in our midst. These were soldiers of our own kingdom of Caskentia, in green uniforms as vibrant as the sprawling valley below. They had occupied the *Argus* since that morning.

This was the second time in as many weeks that my airship had been commandeered. The previous time, rebellious settlers from the Waste had claimed it by force. I rather preferred them. Wasters made for an easy enemy after fifty years of intermittent warfare.

This occupation by our own government was ugly in a different way.

My fists gripped the wheel as if I could leave impressions in the slick copper. The futility of our situation infuriated me. I couldn't stop the Wasters before. And now I couldn't stop *this*, whatever this mysterious errand was.

My son, Sheridan, was on board somewhere. I needed him to be safe, not snared in any more political drama. The Wasters had used him as a hostage to force my hand; I didn't want these soldiers to do the same.

"Captain Hue, sir." My co-pilot saluted as he entered the control cabin. I assessed him in a glance. Bandages plugged his swollen nose. Blood still thickened his thin brown moustache.

"You are well enough to resume your duties?" I asked.

"Yes, sir. I've felt worse after a night of leave."

Ramsay knew his job; if only he could control his fool lips. I stepped back to grant him control of the rudder and leaned by his ear. "Corrado said this would be over in days. Bear through."

I saw my own frustration mirrored in his eyes, and in the other crew as I walked from station to station. I muttered what assurance I could and exited the control cabin. I needed to find my boy.

I limped down the hallway, my stiff knees like smoldering coals of pain. An engineer fresh from the outdoor engine car saluted as she passed by. The stench of enchanted aether-helium clung to her like a cloud and made me woozy for all of a breath.

I started upstairs. Agony compounded with every step. I gritted my teeth. I glanced up at the sound of distinctly heavy boots coming downstairs. Another Caskentian soldier in a green greatcoat and jodhpurs marched toward me. Behind him came Julius Corrado, a man who was no gentleman and deserved no respectful designation.

I'd known Corrado years ago as a smarmy airship port warden, the kind who demanded extra bribes and acted like he'd done me a grand favor. He had aged as well as an apple left out in summer sun—his face and jowls wrinkled and lumpy—though the fine threads of his dapper pinstriped suit would have made him presentable to Queen Evandia herself.

This morning he'd flashed a Clockwork Dagger's pin as he requisitioned my ship in the Queen's very name. An urgent mission, he said. My *Argus* was perfect, he said.

Perfect because we were almost fully staffed and in better condition than most of the ships currently on moorage. I took pride in my old gal. We had spent the past few days replacing blood-soaked carpet and repairing other damage from the Waster skirmish so that we could resume our usual passenger route.

Corrado gave me one of his insipid smiles. "Off duty, Cuthbert?"

My fists balled at my sides. As a younger man,

fancying myself a pugilist, I might have been fool enough to take the punch, but I now had to think of my Sheridan, and two dozen crew besides.

"Off duty as much as a captain ever is."

"I'm on the way to join my man in the control cabin, just to keep an eye on things. Have you seen Mrs. Starling about?"

"No." Damned if I cared. I needed to find my lad. He was most likely in the promenade, and failing that, up in the gas bag access where he liked to read.

"I'm sure she'll turn up soon. She's always up to something." With a tip of his black trilby, he continued downstairs. I grimaced as I headed upward. The Wasters had pummeled me when I resisted their takeover of the *Argus*; my legs had taken the worst of it. Now I moved like an old man. I *felt* like an old man for the first time, despite years of white hair and wrinkles.

Most of the lights in the promenade were shut off, though sun shone through the long row of port-side windows. The view beyond showed the greenery of Caskentia. Set dining tables wore white tablecloths as if to masquerade as squat ghosts.

I heard Sheridan's voice, still high as a girl's, and stopped in the doorway.

"Yes, m'lady, I've officially been yeoman electrician on board for years, but I work where I'm needed."

"Well, you've done a fine job on this automaton band. These figures are far older than you, but they're in fine condition."

It took me a moment to find the speaker, as Mrs.

Starling wore a black mourning gown from nape to ankle and stood in a shadow between windows. In that attire, she'd blend in anywhere in Caskentia. Widows and mourning mothers were legion.

"Thank you, m'lady," said Sheridan.

"Are you reading these books now?" I heard the flutter of pages. My sense of alarm blared like klaxons. I knew nothing about this woman but her name and that she traveled with Corrado. I assumed no innocence on her part.

"I've read them before, m'lady. They're favorites of mine." My Sheridan, never without books. When he first came aboard at age nine, I berated him for reading on duty. I did not hold with nepotism.

"It's rare to find a boy your age who can read, much less one who favors Dhalgren's poetry or histories of Caskentia."

"I credit my mother, m'lady. She was fond of books."

"Such a tragedy to lose your mother at such a tender age. You were what, nine, when she succumbed to pox?"

He hesitated, and my own breath caught in surprise. How had she known that? My crew wouldn't have gossiped about such an intimate detail.

"Yes, m'lady," Sheridan said slowly.

Just weeks before, I read in the paper of Caskentia burning whole villages to contain the spread of pox. Ill and healthy, immolated together. It was a firebreak strategy, a damn fool one. By Caskentia's "death village" logic, Sheridan should be dead, too, even though he never contracted the dreadful illness from his mother.

Caskentia. Logic. Those words shouldn't be used in the same sentence.

It'd shock my crew if I said such things aloud. I displayed absolute loyalty to Caskentia, but I was no fool. I did whatever was necessary to manage my business—my ship—and take care of Sheridan. I paid bribes to officials at every moorage. I simpered and groveled, and in the privacy of my berth, washed away the foul taint with a tawny port.

Maybe that's why this requisition of my gal *Argus* was especially aggravating. All my posturing had been for nothing.

"Mothers are often our best teachers, though your father's role in recent years is not to be ignored. You've raised an intelligent son, Captain Hue." She still faced away from me. Had I been so loud in my approach?

Sheridan scrambled to his feet and saluted me. "Sir!" He wore a crimson crew uniform over his lanky form. A scab still stood bold across his neck. I refused to let my mind linger on the memory of a Waster holding a blade to my boy's throat.

I acknowledged Mrs. Starling with a curt nod, which she returned. She had to be near my own age, her hair threaded in silver.

"He's a bright boy and an asset to my crew," I said. I stood the same distance from her as I would from a snake. "Corrado wondered about your whereabouts, Mrs. Starling."

Her tight smile acknowledged my lack of subtlety in getting rid of her. "I suppose he needs my help, as usual. I should get down to the control cabin. Captain." She swept by me. I waited until the doors swung shut before I turned to Sheridan. He straightened his books then hurriedly stooped to reassemble the bellows mechanism for the trumpet automaton.

"How long had she been here?"

"A few minutes, sir. She surprised me." He didn't look impressed by that; he looked unnerved. Good. He needed that fear.

"I don't know who that woman is. I don't know *what* she is, but she's with Corrado. You know what happened the last time we had Clockwork Daggers aboard."

Sheridan nodded. The Queen's spies were either covert heroes of the realm or chief arbiters of Caskentian corruption, depending on who was doing the talking. My opinion was not favorable in light of recent events. The Wasters' takeover of the *Argus* had been complicated by an on-board rivalry between Clockwork Daggers as they argued over the fate of a meddlesome medician, one Octavia Leander.

All of which resulted in that damned Waster holding a blade to Sheridan's throat as they commandeered my ship.

"Did Mrs. Starling hint at our destination?"

"No, sir. By the way, they had us load two large wardrobe boxes when they came aboard, but their personal bags were quite light. A soldier stays near their berths, too."

Good lad. I offered an approving nod. Queen Evandia had her Daggers as spies; I had my Sheridan. "You had best get that automaton together. You're on shift soon, *Mr. Hue.*"

"Aye, *Captain Hue.*" He had never called me "father" or any such synonym. He'd been a chubby toddler screaming, "Captain! Captain!" after me when I would leave him and his mother at the dock.

My gaze traced that nick on his throat as I turned away.

I stopped in the hallway at the juncture of the downward stairs and the corridors to berthing. A large cage against the wall abounded with the twitters and metallic clicks of dozens of mechanical birds; they were another of Sheridan's projects, and a source of great joy for our commercial passengers.

Away from prying eyes, I allowed my body to sag as I leaned on the wall.

"We'll be back on our boring route soon, old gal," I murmured to the *Argus*, giving the panels a pat.

Up until the Waster attack, I thought the *Argus* was the safest place for Sheridan. Now? I didn't know. The fight between Caskentia and the Waste had continued in fits and starts for decades—recent events on the *Argus* were proof of that—and certainly the full war would resume by spring.

Another year, and Sheridan would be of age for army conscription; I'd already saved up funds for the hefty bribes to keep him off the rosters.

And now Mrs. Starling inquired after him. I dared

not assume she made pleasant maternal chitchat to pass the time. No.

Gravity helped my stiff legs down the stairs and toward the control cabin. I didn't know how to do it, but I needed Corrado, Starling, and their ilk off of my *Argus* as soon as possible.

No good could come of having a Clockwork Dagger aboard my ship.

The night passed, then another day. We continued along the same heading north through Caskentia. Marshes and farmland patched the valley below, the ocean out of sight to the west. At starboard, the high wall of the Pinnacles grew bolder and bleaker with snow. Beyond that fearsome natural border sprawled the desolate plains of the Waste. Hell, if ever there was one.

The next morning, with me at the rudder, Corrado directed us toward a specific location. We were on the far eastern edge of the North Country, a stretch of rolling plains and isolated farms. Not a place to expect a mooring mast, but by God, there was one. It stood like a steel lighthouse. At its feet lay a black slate of rubble freckled with soldiers in Caskentian green.

I stared down through the wide cabin windows. This looked like a pox-ridden death village. The yonder green hills added a splash of color to what otherwise resembled the desolate black print photograph that had accompanied the newspaper story weeks before.

Soldiers assisted as we moored the *Argus* to the top of the mast.

Corrado motioned to me. "Your crew is to stay aboard with the exception of your three aether magi. They'll leave the ship now. Our soldiers are rounding them up."

Jaws dropped across the cabin.

"The hell they are." Spittle sprayed from my lips. "Do you know what you're doing? Aether magi are more accurate than any dial in monitoring our helium and aether mix, and if we're forced to go down, their ability to float obj—"

"I'm well aware of what aether magi do, but they are disembarking nevertheless. If any of them attempt to hide on board, we'll know." His voice brooked no argument. "You conducted thorough maintenance in the past week. Your airship can fly perfectly well without them."

Leaving our aether magi behind was like heading for a mountain hike on a winter day without a good coat. The weather might look fine for now, sure, but it was a damned fool risk to take.

"We can't tarry. We need the magi away while we're still upwind," murmured Mrs. Starling from where she stood in the navigation portion of the cabin.

Corrado nodded. "The magi will be driven to Vorana, where your ship can meet them once our errand is done."

"How far will we need to fly without them?" I asked between clenched teeth. On the ground directly below the control cabin, soldiers escorted my three magi into the village.

"As far as needed," snapped Corrado. A soldier stood wary at his side.

Mrs. Starling whispered something to another of their men, who immediately left.

"These are my crew," I said. "If you're idiotic enough to send them away, grant me a chance to give them a proper farewell."

My co-pilot shot me a look of warning. His swollen face acted as testament to what would happen if I was too lippy.

Mrs. Starling thoughtfully hummed. "Yes, Captain. Say your farewells." She looked at the rest of the crew. "We will disembark for mere minutes. Your captain will be with us. Lest you get any ideas about an early departure, I want you to note the anti-airship gunnery below." She punctuated that with a prim smile.

I looked between her and Corrado. Who was really in charge here?

Stairs curled down the mooring mast. No smoke rose from the ruins, though the strong stench of ashes told me it was razed recently. I counted at least two dozen troops below, and full crews on the gunnery. Why in bloody hell was the Caskentian army guarding this place? What were we doing here?

My magi awaited near a wagon, their hastily packed belongings stuffed in the back. A soldier from my ship watched over them.

"Captain!" cried a magus. They gathered around me.

"Sir!"

"What the hell—"

I raised a hand. "You know I'd never force you off the ship, had I my druthers. I'm not that stupid."

I met their bewildered and angered gazes. "I can't blame you if you take on other jobs in Vorana, but here." I reached into my pocket and offered gilly coins to each of them. "If you still want on with us, I'll look for you at the Hotel Nennia. Damned if I know when we'll get there, though."

"Where's the boy?" called Mrs. Starling as she came up behind me.

"I couldn't find him," said one of the soldiers who'd been aboard the *Argus*.

"Boy?" I snapped, whirling around. "You can't mean—"

She scowled and made an abrupt motion to another soldier. "Go aboard. Hurry. There's a thirteen-year-old boy—"

I stepped forward, fists clenching.

Mrs. Starling faced me, expression cool. "Your son is bright and his potential shouldn't be stymied. He'll depart with the magi. I have a great opportunity in mind for him."

"He's my son, you—"

Corrado blocked me with his body. We stood eye to eye. "It's for the best, Cuthbert. This mission we're undertaking . . . it has risks."

My mouth opened and closed. I wanted my son

with me. I wouldn't trust Corrado and Starling with so much as a piece of pie. "Why? What's this opportunity for him? *Where are we going?*"

"I'll answer the latter as soon as we leave."

The soldiers' boots drummed up the metal staircase of the mooring mast. The *Argus* hovered at the top, the long silver underbelly of her gondola exposed and vulnerable. I rubbed my jaw. No aether magi aboard. No idea if there were mooring masts at our destination; airships didn't land on the ground, they *crashed*. No clue what they planned to do with Sheridan. No way to fight back unless I intended suicide.

"For Caskentia's sake, we must hurry." Mrs. Starling bustled toward the center of the village, motioning us forward; I hung back, an eye on the mast.

She advanced to an area thick with building debris. It wasn't until I was up close that I recognized it contained a macabre basket weave of charred bodies. Hundreds of people, surely. The way the blackened skeletons stacked at the crumbled outer walls ... good God. Had they been alive when the fire was set, and clambered to escape? I'd seen the aftermath of fire-bombings in the war, but never bodies concentrated, tangled, like this.

Scorched bones and rubble snapped under Mrs. Starling's feet as she plowed forward, ash puffing in the air as if she stomped through spilled flour. With one hand, she hitched her skirt to knee level as she paced in a small circle, grimacing.

"Oh, bother," she said, sighing. "I can sense it, but where . . . Ah, here we are." She brushed debris aside to pick up an iridescent white brick.

"The box held up well," said Corrado.

"Of course. It's endured this dozens of times over. We'd planned a few more, but well. Opportunity." A sudden wind billowed ash over us as she stomped out into the road. Her gloved hands brushed off the box, though it seemed strangely clean. Its alabaster surface gleamed and wavered like glass, flawless except for the shallow bevel of the lid.

As I stared at the box, a cold sensation slithered down my spine. Suddenly, I heard compounded screams, yells, and cries, as if they were bound within that warped surface. I retreated several steps, scarcely checking my own urge to scream, as if the horror was contagious. I could imagine falling to my knees as the fire consumed me, ate my flesh—and it didn't stop. As if I were immortal, my pain infinite.

I forced my gaze away, and suddenly the world was fully there again, my breaths ragged to my own ears. I heard heavy breaths from Corrado and the nearest soldiers, too, all of us sounding as though we had run across a field in full military gear. The breeze dried thick sweat on my brow and I realized we all stood downwind of Mrs. Starling. She had not reacted at all.

I was not particularly sensitive to magic. I'd known the heat of a medician's healing circle a few times, and seen infernal magi call up fire. Dark magic was the stuff children whispered about to keep siblings awake long past midnight. I had never considered that it might be real.

"What would happen if that were opened?" I asked, voice rasping.

Mrs. Starling draped a black cloth over the box and the horrid *presence* of it was abruptly muffled. More magic. She tucked the bundle beneath her arm like mere groceries. "Now, Captain Hue, don't ask questions unless you want answers." With that properly schoolmarmish reply, she headed toward the tower.

The noise of wheels made me turn. The wagon with my magi was leaving. At this distance, I couldn't see my boy in the back. I needed to see him, to talk to him. *I needed him.* I lurched into a run, each stride scorching pain up both my knees.

Corrado huffed as he easily caught up with me. "Cuthbert, stop. *Stop.*" He gripped my arm to force me from my vain pursuit. "Let him go. He'll be better off. We must fly on. We can stop the war, Cuthbert. Save your son and generations to come."

Save my son. Stop the war.

Corrado blotted his face with a kerchief—a result of that foul box more than his brief run. He cast a nervous glance toward the tower and Mrs. Starling. "I shouldn't tell you this, but I think you should know. Your ship has been granted a noble task. *You've* been granted a noble task." A sort of religious fervor gleamed in his eyes. "When we open that white box on the far side of the Pinnacles, the Waste will be poisoned. The people, the land. Everything touched by the enchantment."

I stared at him in sick fascination. That small box could do that? I didn't want to believe it, but I couldn't help but shudder.

"Cuthbert, when you were docked in Mercia, did you hear rumors of the Lady's Tree suddenly becoming visible in the southern Waste, revealing a Wasters' settlement at its roots?"

"Certainly." Medicians were said to worship the giant tree; certainly no educated person believed the thing to be *real* before this past week. "Last scuttlebutt I heard was that Caskentia's airship bombardment failed to eliminate the town for some reason, but . . ."

Corrado nodded. "Now you understand."

This doom box was their failsafe, a way to take care of the Waster menace once and for all. "What if that thing is opened on my ship?"

"It won't be. Only a special magus can unlock it. It's just . . . unpleasant for almost everyone else in close proximity. To magi, it's particularly potent. Maddening. It would have been highly disturbing for the crew to witness." He couldn't suppress a shudder of his own.

"Wait—you expect us to get you to the far side of the Pinnacles?"

"No, just . . ." A soldier approached, and Corrado's demeanor abruptly changed. "Just think," he muttered so low I could barely hear. "Caskentia will know peace, because of you."

"Peace." I repeated the word dully as I tried to absorb all he had said. The war had dragged on since I was in knickerbockers. What did I know of peace?

The one mercy was that Sheridan would be far from that vile box, but what opportunity did Mrs. Starling intend for him? When would I see my boy again?

I knew the heavy weight of despair as I trudged up the mast.

"What do you mean, you couldn't find him?" Mrs. Starling's high voice carried down from the top of the tower. I froze.

"We searched the whole ship, m'lady. I'm sorry."

I forced my legs faster up the last flight of stairs. Mrs. Starling lingered at the ramp to the *Argus*. "My son?" I asked.

Winds whipped her black attire. "He's apparently hidden himself aboard. Well, we can't tarry." Mrs. Starling sighed as she glanced at the *Argus* directly above. "What a waste." With that, she advanced up the ramp.

I took a steadying breath as relief and fear flooded through me. I hesitated a few seconds more to regain full composure, then followed her aboard.

I supervised the control cabin as we unmoored and resumed flight. Corrado informed us of our next destination.

"The northern pass." I stared at him. "The first snow of the season just—"

"It's not fully winter yet, and the *Argus* doesn't need to fly all the way to the Waste, just to the divide, then you can return to Caskentia."

My crew shifted and glanced around, dread and fear thick in the air. Two soldiers stood feet away in the navigation section of the cabin; three more were aboard elsewhere. Fewer soldiers than before, but the threat of their presence remained palpable.

At least Mrs. Starling wasn't in the cabin. I didn't want that damned box anywhere near my officers on duty, even if that cloth around it somehow smothered its power.

"Do you have a mooring mast at the divide as well?" I asked Corrado. "Or are we tenderly booting you out the freight ramp?"

"I'm touched that you'd do so tenderly."

"My concern is for my crew and my ship." Sheridan. Where was that boy hiding? *Why* was he hiding? "Even going halfway through the pass is a damned risk—"

"Caskentia requires your service. Get us to the divide. We'll take care of ourselves from there."

I'd been known to gamble at times, but even with a million gilly coins up for wager, I would not have flown his proposed route at this time of year.

I looked to Yee, my officer on watch; Ramsay at the rudder wheel; Jonah at the elevator panel; my navigator, and all the rest. I had twenty crew on board, most with family. I pressed a hand to the wall to keep my posture strong even as my legs screamed agony.

Old gal, I wanted to tell the ship, *you deserve a better grave than the godforsaken Pinnacles. All of us do.*

"Operate as normal into the northern pass." Corrado motioned to his remaining men as he left. The two Caskentian soldiers stood ready and wary.

Operate as normal, indeed. What a piss-poor kind of normal.

I met eyes all around the room. "You heard the man. You know our aether magi are absent. I want a double shift to monitor our gas levels. Yee, any word on the whereabouts of Mr. Hue?"

"No, sir," Yee said, her brown skin blanched. "Soldiers searched the whole ship. He never went down the mast."

"Spread the word that our yeoman electrician should carry on with his duties." Much as I wanted to treat him as my son, right now, shorthanded as we were, I needed him more as crew. "He's stuck on board with us now."

Officer Yee saluted. "Yes, Captain."

We flew onward. I spent the next hours with my navigator as we reviewed our most current weather maps and plotted our course and elevation.

"Sir?" murmured the navigator, a wary eye to the nearest soldier. "Whatever this mission is, they don't want us alive to tell tales, do they?"

I opened and closed my mouth without speaking, realizing the man was terrified and needed to talk.

He rambled on, "The wind shears at the divide will chew us like a dog with a bone, and if we survive turning around, we'll have the wind bearing down on our bow the whole flight back. If a storm meets us head-on, it'll be like flying against a hurricane. Our gas bags will shred."

"If we fight back—if we win—that carries risks, too," I muttered.

"Better to fight, sir, than to blithely fly a suicide mission. Maybe then my wife would have something to bury. No one would find our ship on the Pinnacles." A pencil twirled in his shaky grip. "I think that's what they want."

I met his fierce gaze and bowed my head to study our charts again.

After a while, word came to me that Sheridan had emerged and stood his proper watch elsewhere. Restless as I was to see him, I tried to content myself with that knowledge as I busied myself with necessary work to keep us aloft and alive.

The sun set early in the autumnal far north. Stars sparkled on high as we entered the northern pass to the Waste. A grim, sleepless tension clutched the crew, and shift changes did nothing to alleviate that dread.

I departed the cabin and walked to the stairs as I mulled methods to quietly eliminate the soldiers without risking a gun battle on board. Ricochets were a danger with our largely metal interior. I worried for our gas bags directly above deck A as well; a helium vessel such as ours wasn't as inclined to immolate as old hydrogen models, but fire was the greatest enemy to sailors of sea or air.

I recognized the rapid patter of shoes coming downstairs from deck A. *Sheridan*. I wavered on my feet and caught myself on the railing as he came into view. I didn't know if I should shake his hand or throttle him.

"The smoke room," I said, motioning my son downstairs again. The double doors clacked as we entered. The space was empty. Even the cabinets behind the bar were vacant, the liquor locked away in our bartender's absence. "Where did you . . . ?"

"I heard a soldier asking after me. I hid where they never thought to look—Corrado's berth." I shook my head at his cleverness. "I broke into his wardrobe box, then Mrs. Starling's. They have two wing suits. The real deal."

We'd seen some suits in action back in summer. They were a newfangled invention out of Tamarania, a sort of backpack with broad, fold-out wings. I called them a stylish form of suicide.

Suddenly, everything made sense. "Corrado ordered us to fly to the divide in the northern pass. Now I understand why. With the wind behind them, the petrol in those wing suits would be adequate to fly them to Caskentia's encampment on the far side. They'd manage the shears better than an airship." I rubbed my bristled jaw. "You should know what happened in the village, Mr. Hue." I recounted the events from the ground.

"Captain, in the really old stories they say the Waste is called the Waste because Caskentia's magi cast a blood spell a thousand years ago that made the land infertile and the settlers sick. It sounds like Mr. Corrado and Mrs. Starling intend to recreate that."

How many villages had been burned in the name of pox containment? Had they even *had* pox at all, or were they all deemed a sacrifice—an offering—for this enchantment?

The *Argus* was being offered for the cause, too.

I hated Wasters as much as anyone. They damn near killed my Sheridan. But I knew what I felt standing near that atrocious box. Could I wish that darkness on anyone, Waster or Caskentian? Even if it ended the war?

Even if it did bring about lasting peace, Sheridan wouldn't be alive to enjoy it.

As I mulled possibilities, a bell toned from down the hall. The engine-car-personnel shift change was done. Inspiration struck. My head jerked up.

"Aether gas," I said. Mechanics stationed in the engine cars required full gas masks to stay conscious amidst the enchanted gas.

"Sir?"

"We need to subdue the soldiers without gunfire. Get our spare gas masks—"

"Oh, yes! Saturate the filters in aether, force them to breathe through the masks. It'll work, sir!" He almost bounced in excitement. "I'll inform the rest of the crew—"

"No." I stopped him with an outstretched hand as I thought on my discussion with our navigator. "We need to ask them first. If we succeed and survive, life afterward will not be easy." Sheridan looked at me blankly. I sighed. "This is sedition, Mr. Hue. We're not merely subverting the command of a Clockwork Dagger, but Queen Evandia herself. Recollect the so-called traitors we often see hanged near ports. Many of them die on hearsay alone. How will we be judged?"

"Oh." His Adam's apple bobbed as he swallowed. "What if we do as they ask and fly to the divide? Is there *any* chance we could make it home, sir?"

"Mr. Hue, anything is possible, but I've heard drunken airship crews in taverns across Caskentia boast many things, and I have never heard anyone claim to have flown that far into the northern pass and back to Caskentia at this time of year. Dragon sightings are more believable."

"I see, sir." He looked fearful but resolute. "I'll quietly consult the crew."

I clasped his shoulder. "As will I. God willing, we can regain full control of the *Argus* before it's too late, Mr. Hue."

For all that there were fewer soldiers aboard, they seemed damned near everywhere. They didn't interfere, however, as I made my usual rounds. Wherever privacy allowed, I briefed my crew on the situation. All agreed to fight our occupation. I returned to the control cabin to wait as Sheridan set the plot in motion.

High winds rattled the *Argus*, though they favored us for now. I stared out the broad windows of the bow and into the bleak night. The deep, jagged crevasse stretched before us. Snow glowed beneath moonlight.

A soft noise carried from the hall. Had our insurrection begun? It took all my will not to turn. I didn't dare drag the soldiers' attention with me. A long minute passed.

Then, chaos. More crew dashed in, their movements flurried like a startled flock of gremlins. Yelling, "Get him, get the gun!" "Down!" "Pin him!" "Get the mask on!" A soldier's arm swung out and sent two men flying. Other crew fell like dominoes. More screams. A bullet pinged. My red-attired crew lunged atop the soldiers in a tangle of limbs.

I stood, my legs stiff as if I was turning into a statue. I glanced around. Essential crew positions were still manned.

My crew untwined themselves and stood. I spied the soldiers, their bodies slack. Leather gas masks covered their faces, their visages bug-like. Each mask was quickly removed as other hands worked to secure the soldiers' arms and legs.

"Report! Where'd that bullet go?" I snapped.

The trajectory had taken it through the ballast board, just feet away from Ramsay at the rudder, then through the upper portion of the elevator board, where it again ricocheted. All vital equipment. Ballast was water stored as a weight to counterbalance the loft of gas; we would drop some ballast if we needed to quickly ascend. The elevator controls kept us level.

One of my crew didn't move. Yee, my off-duty watch officer. Blood and brain spattered the floor. The bullet had made a full circuit of the cabin to strike her in the back of the skull.

Grief rocked me, but I had no time to linger on our loss. "Where are the other soldiers? Corrado? Starling?"

"Captain, sir!" A mechanic saluted me. Her nose was bloodied flat, her voice tinny. A soldier lay hogtied at her feet. "The two swaddies in the berths went down easy, but Corrado and Starling put up a fight on the stairs. Not sure what happened to them."

"Soldier in the hall's out, too," said a steward.

Where was Sheridan? Did we have any other casualties? I gritted my teeth. First things first.

"Correct our heading, Ramsay."

Never was I as proud of my crew as at that moment, the way we fought wind shears to steadily bring the *Argus* around. Icy peaks looked sharp enough to pierce the old gal's belly. The wind clawed and buffeted us as we came broadside, then we took it dead-on. The Waste now astern, we pointed toward the green valley of home, still hidden by countless ridges of mountains.

Our elevation was too high.

I stepped closer to the ballast board, just beside my helmsman. The readings looked the same as before, frozen beside the massive dent of the bullet. I looked to Ramsay, who like me had decades of experience on airships.

"The ballast . . ."

"Aye, sir. Damage must have triggered our ballast to release. We're losing water slow-like, but . . ."

In the valley, we kept our maximum elevation at five hundred feet. Here in the pass, at this elevation and with less pressure on our gas bags, we had to take even more care. If we kept rising, our lift gas would expand and we risked gas bag ruptures. Of all the voyages to not have our magi.

"Vent gas as needed. Push us to maximum knots. God willing, we'll make the foothills before our depleted bags force us down." As if the odds against us were not terrible enough.

Leaving the cabin in Ramsay's capable hands, I hurried down the hall as fast as my legs allowed. A good number of crew had gathered at the bottom of the open stairwell. The secured, unconscious soldiers had been dragged downstairs and to one side.

"Captain!" called the chief cook. "The Dagger's here." He pushed aside some of the other men to reveal Corrado by their feet.

He had attired himself in thick coats to survive the deep cold of mountain flight. His mouth gaped, his eyes shut. One of my nearby crew held the wing suit. The heavy unit of slick, curvaceous brass had tall sticks attached to either side that resembled shuttered umbrellas. Heavy leather straps and buckles dragged on the floor.

"Why haven't Corrado's limbs been secured?" I asked.

"I didn't know to take the mask off again right away, sir," a man said, his voice raspy as he shakily saluted me.

"Aether suffocation." I shook my head in disgust. "More merciful than he deserved. You . . ."

"I'm sorry, sir. I didn't think he would die that fast."

He wavered on his feet and I braced him by the shoulder. He was terrified of me, but more terrified of what he had caused. "Corrado was going to kill you, kill all of us. He deserves no grief." His face remained blank, my words unable to pierce his shock. He was a rare Caskentian, to be so unacquainted with death. I turned away. "Where's Starling?"

"She fled toward the hold, sir!" called one of my new hires, a woman steward. "She wore one of them wing suits, too. Mr. Hue and some of the others were right behind."

Mention of Sheridan caused my breath to catch. I motioned to the lollygagging crew. "Keep guards on the soldiers. The rest of you, with me."

We rushed through the crew section, passed our berths, and entered the darkened hold. Large parcels of freight filled the space along with our usual stores. Sheridan hunkered behind a box larger than him, with two other men close by. Farther back in the hold, I heard a distinct and familiar rattle.

"Secure yourselves!" I yelled and lunged to grab the steel ribbing of the wall.

The freight ramp opened with a roar and high whistle of wind. The beleaguered *Argus* shuddered and groaned at the pressure change as cold bludgeoned us. I gripped two security straps fastened to the wall. I quickly looped one through my belt and knotted it, then used the other to hop over to Sheridan as if rappelling. Out of my sight, the metal mouth of the ramp clanged, the wind clattering it shut in bursts. A glance confirmed that the rest of my crew had found handholds and ropes.

"Captain?" called Mrs. Starling. Her voice was faint over the wind and clamor of metal.

"Corrado's dead," I yelled. "We're flying back to Caskentia."

"Idiot! Sabotaging . . . best effort . . . stop the war."

"How many Caskentians died to fuel that box of yours?" I yelled. She surely had it on her person.

"Thousands." I hoped I'd misheard her, but I feared I had not. "You'd . . . vain!"

"Then make it to the Waste, if you can!" I yelled back. "Don't risk our hides." *Don't risk Sheridan.*

I squeezed his arm then passed the rope to his grip. He'd known sailor knots before he knew his letters, so it took him mere seconds to secure the rope to his belt. I gingerly moved past him so I could look around at Starling. The wind and my own accursed stiffness dropped me to a knee. The iciness of the floor stabbed through the cloth.

"You're not going to survive . . . night. Winds . . . Even if you did . . . send Daggers after you. Keep you quiet."

I forced away more grief as I wondered at the fate of my aether magi.

Mrs. Starling stood with her back to the clattering hatch, secured by her own rope. Her body was bundled thick like an autumn bear, the broad straps of the wing suit forming an X over her chest. Over her shoulders, the wings had opened slightly and seemed rigged to her arms by a series of pulleys. A full leather helmet, the goggles glassed in green, covered her head. She poked around some other crates, looking for something. A way to keep the hatch open, I imagined. She couldn't risk it crunching her or the wings.

"With Corrado gone, that's one fewer," I said.

For a moment, I mistook her high laugh for the wind. "I'm the Clockwork Dagger! Corrado . . . assistant . . . damn poor one. Your boy, on the other hand . . ."

"My boy?" I snapped.

" . . . Reputation among docks and crews . . . Clever. Curious. I see one of your men brought Corrado's wings. Give . . . Sheridan. Barely . . . petrol to make the flight. He can come with me . . . train in the palace."

I wanted Sheridan to live out his potential, but I also wanted him to keep his *soul*. I looked at Sheridan. He seemed dumbstruck. God help me, was he actually considering this?

Mrs. Starling continued, "Besides . . . Captain. Feel . . . ship . . . something wrong, not just headwind . . . crash soon . . . he . . . wear wings. Escape."

Faint light shone on Sheridan's smooth face, his slim body. He was still very much a child. "Sheridan?" I whispered. When had I last called to him by his first name?

"No!" He shouted to be heard. I released a breath

deeper than my lungs. "I'm crew of the *Argus*. I will not abandon ship." He met my eye and murmured, "I won't abandon *you*, Captain."

" . . . Very well!" Mrs. Starling's voice rang out. " . . . No second chances . . . Good as damned."

There was a hard clang, then another. I looked around. Mrs. Starling had grabbed a length of rebar and was stabbing it onto the hatch. I knew she'd succeeded to hold the maw wide open when the wind truly howled through and around us, the chill like death. Loose ropes and detritus blew about. An old, desecrated portrait of Queen Evandia—stored down here for ages—flapped past me and toward the hatch.

When I looked around again, Mrs. Starling was gone.

"Sheridan?" I bent close to his face. "You can leave with those wings. Go on your own."

"No, sir." His gaze was hard.

"We've lost our ballast. The *Argus* is venting gas. We're going to crash. The hatch is open now—".

"Sir. No. I can't."

"You can, damn it."

"No, Captain, I *can't*." His voice softened. I leaned closer. "After we spoke, I sneaked into the wardrobe boxes and sabotaged both suits. Hers will glide for a while, but the boosters are dead. There's no uplift or steering."

"Oh, my boy." I laughed, the sound more like a wheeze through my cold-clenched throat. "You out-Daggered the Dagger."

That accursed box would be buried in some high crest where the snow never melted. Maybe, after a time, the enchantment would dissipate and those captured screams would silence.

It took several minutes of precarious teamwork for us to shut the hatch. The hold secure, all of us near frozen solid, we retreated into the ship. The crew saluted me as we entered the control car. Their grins were grim, with reason. We'd vented a great deal of gas to control our ascent, and now skirted a mere hundred feet over the ground.

Dead ahead, the green-sliver of Caskentia shone in the weak dawn light. Clouds thickened the sky. A storm was sweeping in from the ocean. If we'd gone all the way to the divide, our fates would have been guaranteed.

"The old gal is mine," I said to Ramsay at the rudder. "I'll take her down."

The metal wheel was warm from my co-pilot's hold. "Crew, it's been an honor to serve with you tonight. If we live past dawn, Caskentia may well hunt for us to find out what transpired here. It may be a sorry life, but—"

"Pardon, sir," called the navigator. "It'll be a life." Grunts around the cabin backed him up.

"Very well," I said. Sheridan stood beside me, his legs braced. I wanted to order him away from this glass-and-steel cage that would likely crumple upon impact, but I knew he'd disobey. Feeling the pressure of my gaze, he glanced over with a small smile.

Oh, God. He trusted me, that we'd survive.

I gripped the wheel harder, willing my thoughts into the *Argus*.

You've been good to us, old gal. I'll do my best to be kind in these next minutes.

The sunlight from astern illuminated the skies ahead in brilliant purple and grey, the sprawling valley below an unreal, verdant green. I smiled. Views like this were why I'd taken to air as a boy, why I rarely stayed aground long.

What a beautiful, perfect dawn to share with my son.

ACKNOWLEDGMENTS

Each of these works has been published individually, and thus has already had an acknowledgments page. To everyone I already thanked—thank you again! This collection wouldn't exist without your support.

I am forever grateful to my agent, Rebecca Strauss at DeFiore and Company. She plucked my query letter out of the slush pile and has made so many of my dreams come true. I haven't stopped dreaming, either.

I will forever be flabbergasted by the Nebula nomination for *Wings of Sorrow and Bone*. I'm deeply honored that readers found it worthy. Thank you; I'd feed you all maple cookies if I could.

Lastly, for my husband Jason, my favorite big dork, who knows when to back away slowly when I'm working and does what he can to get vacation days so I can attend conventions. He knows he'll get lots of cookies, too.

ABOUT THE AUTHOR

BETH CATO is the author of the fantasy duology *The Clockwork Dagger*, which was nominated for the Locus Award for Best First Novel, and *The Clockwork Crown*, as well as two short stories and a novella in the Clockwork realm. Her novella, *Wings of Sorrow and Bone*, has been nominated for a Nebula Award. Beth writes and bakes cookies in a lair outside of Phoenix, Arizona, which she shares with a hockey-loving husband, a numbers-obsessed son, and a cat the size of a canned ham.

Discover great authors, exclusive offers, and more at hc.com.